"What do you want?"

Sarah kept her foot braced against the door.

"My...boy here, he's sick." The man laid his hand on the boy's head, drawing her attention to the child.

Scruffy, mud-streaked and shaggy-haired, he stared up at her with his bright blue gaze. The boy—how old? Five, six, maybe?—didn't lean on his father, didn't seem connected to him.

She sighed and unhooked the chain. "I'm unlocking the door." She motioned to the boy. "He can come in. You—" she jerked her head toward the man "—stay outside."

At her words, the child turned to his father and tugged on the man's washed-out jeans. Sarah stared at the two faces that were so different from each other.

The boy didn't look like his father. But who could really tell what the father looked like, hidden behind the thick beard and mustache? Was he friend or foe?

Dear Reader:

Happy holidays! Our authors join me in wishing you all the best for a joyful, loving holiday season with your family and friends. And while celebrating the new year—and the new decade!—I hope you'll think of Silhouette Books.

1990 promises to be especially happy here. This year marks our tenth anniversary, and we're planning a celebration! To symbolize the timelessness of love, as well as the modern gift of the tenth anniversary, each month in 1990, we're presenting readers with a *Diamond Jubilee* Silhouette Romance title, penned by one of your all-time favorite Silhouette Romance authors.

In January, under the Silhouette Romance line's *Diamond Jubilee* emblem, look for Diana Palmer's next book in her bestselling LONG, TALL TEXANS series—*Ethan*. He's a hero sure to lasso your heart! And just in time for Valentine's Day, Brittany Young has written *The Ambassador's Daughter*. Spend the most romantic month of the year in France, the setting for this magical classic. Victoria Glenn, Annette Broadrick, Peggy Webb, Dixie Browning, Phyllis Halldorson—to name just a few!—have written *Diamond Jubilee* titles especially for you. And Pepper Adams has penned a trilogy about three very rugged heroes—and their lovely heroines!—set on the plains of Oklahoma. Look for the first book this summer.

The *Diamond Jubilee* celebration is Silhouette Romance's way of saying thanks to you, our readers. We've been together for ten years now, and with the support you've given us, you can look forward to many more years of heartwarming, poignant love stories.

I hope you'll enjoy this book and all of the stories to come. Come home to romance—Silhouette Romance—for always!

Sincerely,

Tara Hughes Gavin
Senior Editor

LINDSAY LONGFORD

Jake's Child

Silhouette *Romance*

Published by Silhouette Books New York

America's Publisher of Contemporary Romance

For Wes, in spite of everything
and because of so much more.

For Robert, my son,
who fills my world with sunshine.

For Ann Reynolds,
the best sister in the world.

And for Jan Milella,
whose generous heart, loving spirit
and courage make the world a better place.

SILHOUETTE BOOKS
300 E. 42nd St., New York, N.Y. 10017

ISBN: 0-373-08696-2

First Silhouette Books printing January 1990

Printed in the U.S.A.

LINDSAY LONGFORD's

biggest writing influence has been, as with so many others, her love of reading. She says she'd read toothpaste labels just to have something to read! After studying fiction writing at Northwestern University and writing numerous short stories, she discovered that what she really liked to write was the kind of story she chose when she was tired, wanted a lift or just wanted to be swept away for a few hours—romance.

Her husband has been a constant source of encouragement, and with their ten-year-old-son, they cross-country ski, hit the cinemas once a week and try not to overload their house with too many books.

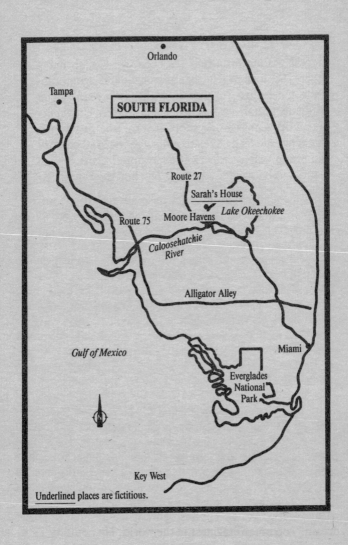

Orlando

Tampa

SOUTH FLORIDA

Route 27

Sarah's House

Route 75   Moore Havens   *Lake Okeechokee*

Caloosehatchie River

Alligator Alley

Gulf of Mexico

Miami

Everglades National Park

N

Key West

Underlined places are fictitious.

Chapter One

The pounding on the screen door woke her up just before midnight.

Her heart banged against her ribs, and for a moment Sarah couldn't remember where she was. A hazy, dreamy memory of happiness lingered, confusing her with its promise. Looking down at her hands clenched in the pilled blue knit of the afghan, she saw that sometime in the night she'd pulled it up over her legs. The wind must have risen out on the lake. Surely no one was going out fishing now.

The screen door rattled as a fist beat on its frame. Whoever was out there wanted in.

Sarah pulled the afghan up closer to her neck and curled her bare legs, clad in cutoff shorts, under her. Late-night fishermen were crazy, swarming out on Okeechobee for catfish. Her regulars knew they needed reservations to go catfishing or crab gigging. None of them would show up at this time of night hoping for a boat and bait.

She rubbed her eyes, chasing away the remnants of her dream. Too much craziness in the world. He could just stay there in the swampy darkness. He didn't know she was inside.

Outside, the latch on the screen door of the wraparound porch squeaked as a hand tugged hard on the handle.

Would he break in if he thought no one was home? Sarah poked her finger through a hole in the blue yarn. She swallowed. The lake was overrun with strangers these days, drug runners, alligator poachers, scum of all kind. Maybe she'd had enough of the solitude and loneliness of Okeechobee. Maybe she needed to be around people again. Sarah shook her head, trying to wake up, reluctant to shed the illusory comfort of her dream.

The thump of booted feet on the old boards of the porch jerked her to her feet.

Under the yellow porch light, shadows moved toward her front door. Sarah reached under the sofa where she'd been half sitting, half lying, for the baseball bat she kept there. Gripping it, she breathed deeply and eased off the sofa. Her bare feet touched the cool wood floor and slid silently across planks worn smooth over the years. She edged to the door separating her from the screened porch.

"Hey! Anybody home?" The voice was a whiskey-roughened rasp sawing through the night.

Sarah stopped. Eerily lit by the yellow light, a large hand rubbed a pane of the floor-to-ceiling windows facing the porch and a blurred face peered in at her. She'd forgotten her glasses. Damn. Holding the bat in her hand, flexing the weighted end, she stood for a moment thinking. Like a wild creature she remained motionless, waiting for the hunter's movement to signal that she'd been spotted.

Maybe he'd go away.

The heel of that large hand whacked hard just above the front-door knob. She heard a curse.

And then a higher sound, a child's voice. "We ain't gonna get in."

"Yeah, we are." The deeper voice was chilling in its matter-of-fact certainty.

Sarah's fists pressed hard against her chest, the bat knocked against her knees. *A child's voice.*

Drawn irresistibly to the door, she pressed her hot face against its coolness, her cheek absorbing the shudder of the fist pounding on wood panels. She'd be a fool, a damn fool to open the door.

She knew better. People, especially women living by themselves, didn't open doors to strangers. She'd lived out here too long to be that stupid. After dark dropped its curtain on the lake, night creatures came out. Smart folks stayed home behind closed and locked doors. Boats disappeared on the lake, cars vanished from the long, lonely sweep of Alligator Alley slicing across the state, and water-bleached bodies bobbed up unexpectedly in weed-clogged shallows and saw grass. No, she knew better than to open her door and invite in danger.

The booted feet shifted, floorboards creaked, and again Sarah heard that childish voice.

"... hurts bad now."

The thin treble halted the awful pounding that vibrated through the door to her body. Hearing the voice, she felt an old wound twisting and turning deep inside her. Sarah flinched.

Bracing her foot against the door, she cracked it open. With the bat at her side, she looked out into the night.

A rush of damp air, smelling of sea things and secrets, swept through the opening.

The hairy, angry face looking back at her was every woman's nightmare.

Sarah tried to slam the door shut, and the man's open palm slapped against the edge, forcing it against the chain's length. His eyes glinted in the yellow light as he kept his palm there, telling her more clearly than words her chain couldn't keep him out.

Sarah leaned her shoulder on the door. "We're closed! Go away. No fishing tonight!" She raised the bat, a puny threat against the strength of those fingers gripping the edge of the door. She pushed. "I said the camp is closed." Shoving against that steady pressure from outside, she pressed her hip into the door.

She'd been a fool, after all. Under the trees the stranger's rusty pickup truck sagged in the sandy earth. In the sudden still of the night, she saw and heard everything with a frightening clarity: details like the man's square fingers with their even nails, the sound of her own quickened breathing, the small shape at the man's side, all registered in her brain.

"Look, give me a minute, will you?" The man's impatience colored his deep voice. He shifted, but his fingers stayed clamped on the door.

Sarah felt the easing of pressure and kept her foot braced against a sudden move. "What do you want? It's late. Come back tomorrow." Tension tightened her throat.

The fingers curled around the door, dropped to the man's side. "My...boy here, he needs to use a bathroom."

"A bathroom?" Sarah started shaking her head. "He can go outside."

"He's sick." Never taking his light brown eyes from hers, the man laid his hand on the boy's head, drawing her attention to the child.

Scruffy, mud-streaked and shaggy-haired, the child wasn't appealing. Bright blue eyes in a sharp-pointed face gleamed with too much knowledge learned too early, and those eyes assessed her with the intelligence and alertness of an adult as he waited impassively with the man for her decision.

The boy—how old? Five, six, maybe?—didn't lean on his father, didn't seem connected to him. Sarah moved to get a better look at both of them. The man's hand had slipped to the boy's neck and rested there in either a caress or a threat.

She looked into the man's strange, pale eyes again, trying to decide. Brown eyes should be deep and rich, warm. Glittering with the force his body only hinted at, these brown eyes were cold. They judged her and sentenced her while something glimmered in their paleness like the silver shine of a minnow in the sunlight.

"Let's go," the boy whispered. "I told you she ain't gonna let us in."

"I got a sick kid here," the man insisted, irritation surfacing in his voice. "I saw your sign out on the road." His forefinger and thumb tipped the boy's head from side to side in a gentle movement. "We've been driving all day and he just started complaining of stomach cramps."

"I don't have public facilities." Sarah turned away. She inched the door forward, the chain drooping now. Half expecting a shove against the door, she almost missed the small movement of the boy.

His sudden stir, one ragged sneaker crossing over the other, was every child's universal signal of dire and immediate need. His face went greenish-white.

Sarah sighed and unhooked the chain. If the man pushed, she'd slam the door on his hand. "I'm unlocking the door. He," she motioned to the boy, "can come in. You," she jerked her head toward the man, "stay outside."

At her words, the boy turned to his father and tugged on the man's washed-out jeans. He bent down, his size hiding the boy's whispered comment from her. Straightening, the man looked at her for a second, deciding something before speaking. He glanced at the child and back up to her. The boy now clutched the man's hand. Sarah looked at the two faces, so different from each other. The boy didn't look like his father, but who could really tell what the father looked like, hidden as he was behind the thicket of beard and moustache?

His voice grainy with satisfaction at her expense, the man smiled thinly. "My boy doesn't want to come in by himself."

"Well, he'll have to go outside, then." Sarah hated the coldness in her voice. But it wouldn't hurt the boy to go in the bushes.

The boy pulled on his father's hand. The boy's bright blue eyes met hers with quick shame.

"Look, the kid's got stomach flu or something. You going to make him throw up in the bushes with the snakes?"

He was afraid! This tough little nut with the streetwise face was afraid of the outdoors even with his father beside him.

Odd child. In Florida's back country, kids grew up used to swamp and snakes. This unkempt duo looked like backwoods, but the boy couldn't be. His foot rubbed on the toe of his sneaker. Sarah didn't like the look of humiliation and desperation he gave her. It made her feel small and mean.

"Jake, I'm gonna—" The boy's anguished wail had the man stooping down to lift him.

"As a matter of fact, lady, he's just about to throw up all over your front porch, so make up your mind fast!" The man's lips drew back in a snarl.

She couldn't slam her door on that sick little face with its shamed eyes. She couldn't do that. She wished she could, though. She didn't want the man or his son in her house for any reason.

Well, prudence and self-respect didn't always walk hand in hand. Sarah swung the living room door open.

"All right. The bathroom's over there." She gestured with the bat, making sure the man noted it now if he'd missed it earlier. She stayed by the open door. She could always take off into the darkness and find a hiding place.

The man looked at her as if he'd read her thoughts. Again a shadow of amusement and something else shone in his clear brown eyes. "C'mon, Nicholas." They headed to the dark door Sarah indicated.

She cleared her throat, annoyed with herself that she'd let them into her home. "Switch is on the right." Light flooded into the living room from the half-open bathroom door. Low murmurs she couldn't hear tantalized her, but she stayed near the door.

She didn't want to know about them, this strange child and his puzzlingly angry father who didn't even look like him. Placing the bat in her other hand, she wondered what was taking so long. Surely a small male person could handle his business with a little more dispatch? Males were better equipped to be more efficient about bathrooms, after all.

The toilet flushed. The rough voice mumbled something, and then Sarah heard water swish in the basin. Another mumble and the gurgle of sink water.

"Okay, Nicholas. Turn off the light." The click was loud in the silent room.

They came out, the boy rubbing his eyes and the man looking down at the boy and then back at her with obvious hostility.

In the light Sarah could see that they were tired, not filthy. The boy's eyes were red-rimmed, with a near-the-edge look of exhaustion. The man was in marginally better shape, though the merciless light did nothing to remove his air of menace. He loomed before her, looking even more frightening in the light than the dark.

Clean, washed-out jeans and wool shirt flowed over a tough body. His muscular shoulders sloped into biceps and forearms the strength of which she'd already experienced. Drops of water clung to shiny, dark hair where he'd slicked it back off his forehead and down to his strongly corded neck. She'd never felt comfortable around big men, and this man typified everything masculine she didn't like. Hairy, rough, aggressive. Too sure of himself.

His eyes, though, were like the lake in summer when the water level dropped and the water gleamed sherry-bright and clear, not like the dark winter depths that lured and betrayed fishermen out too far. She forgot to be afraid when she looked into this man's eyes.

"There. You survived, lady. Wasn't too painful, was it?"

Sarah swung the bat lazily. "Don't get nasty. It suits you, though," she dared, narrowing her eyes. At the man's frown, she rushed on. "Well, glad I could help out." Opening the door wide, she made her intention unmistakable.

Nobody moved. Two pairs of very different eyes met hers steadily: the blue eyes glazed over with fatigue; the brown ones challenging her. Once more fear slithered through her.

Now what? "That's that, then." She tightened her lips into a smile.

Again the boy tugged on the jeans and the big body bent down. Again the low murmurs. The man folded his arms over his chest and glared at her. "The kid wants a cookie. Can't you give him a cookie first?"

"A cookie?" Sarah's mouth dropped open. He expected her to hand out cookies? To a sick child? At this time of night? But his expression clearly said that, by God, she'd better come up with a cookie or else. "I don't have any cookies! Anyway, he's sick. He shouldn't be eating cookies." She inched to the door. The man was clearly unhinged. Her lips caught on dry teeth as she tried to smile. "You'd be welcome, of course, if I had any. Cookies, that is. Really, you would be," she insisted as he shifted his weight.

Sarah stretched one hand in back of her, straining for the door so that she could slam it behind her as she raced into the night. She'd turn off the light outside, too, leaving him blind in unfamiliar country.

He still hadn't moved, but she felt as though he surrounded her.

She raised the bat.

"For God's sake, you got a bee in your brain? Quit waving that damn fool bat at me and settle down, okay?" Tall, dark and hairy flicked the bat out of her hand and closed the door. "Look, we've been driving all day and the kid's tired and hungry. I guess you're right about the cookie, but he's just heaved up everything he's eaten today. Don't you have anything that would settle his stomach?" The man banged the bat on the floor.

Sarah heard the boy's whispered, "It's all right, Jake."

The angry reply was loud in the silence. "I'll get you food, Nicholas. It's the least she can do."

The man called Jake swung towards her, the bat forgotten in his large hand, and a surge of terror rose in Sarah like bile. Why had she ever opened that now-closed door? Was she going to be killed over a stupid cookie?

"Don't, Jake. I'm not real hungry."

Sarah looked at the boy's pinched face and the bruised shadows under his eyes. Reluctantly, in spite of her best intentions, she spoke. "I have some bread, crackers." Frantically she ransacked her brain. "Maybe chicken soup?"

The boy shrugged his shoulders.

"You, too, Jake? It's Jake, isn't it?" At his blank expression, she rattled on. "Yes, of course, Jake." She led them to the kitchen. Knives, a back door.

From the corner of her eye, she saw the boy's wide-eyed stare. "Sure, ma'am. I'd like soup. Right, Jake?" Again he tugged on Jake's faded jeans.

With the ease of long familiarity in the dark, she walked straight to the icebox. Everybody in her family had always called it the icebox. Right now, thinking of all the people who'd lived here helped her believe she might survive this night. The small bulb shone on her shaking hands as she reached inside for soda and bread.

"You here alone?" Jake flipped the light switch.

"Not for long," she lied, throwing a quick glance over her shoulder. He was too close. She must be panicked. She'd never even thought about turning on the light in her desire to reach the safety of the kitchen.

Now she was trapped. He dropped into the seat nearest the back door. She couldn't get to the door without passing dangerously close to him.

The boy—Nicholas?—scooted onto the seat next to the man and watched her. Interest chased the glaze of fatigue from the boy's eyes. "Need some help, ma'am?"

If he were a dog, his whole body would have shaken with the force of his enthusiasm. She didn't smile at him, didn't encourage his reaching out, but she felt like a real stinker when he looked away. She'd seen the flash of awareness in those young-old eyes.

She swallowed. The fear the man's presence aroused in her didn't justify treating the boy the way she had. Not his fault. If both of them would ... would just leave. The boy drummed his heels on the rung of the chair.

"Be still, Nicholas." Jake's level voice stopped the restless movement.

Unnaturally obedient, Nicholas folded his hands together and laid his head down. His eyes followed her every movement. Sarah was irritated with herself. She slapped the table knife hard on the dry toast. Even in a situation like this a little kindness wouldn't kill her. Well, it might, but if it didn't she was going to remember that child's face for the rest of her life. One more portrait for her nightmare gallery.

Grudgingly she turned, meeting the man's unsettling brown eyes for only an instant, and spoke to the boy as she dumped canned soup into a pot. "You can get jelly if you want some."

The boy looked to his father—how different they looked—for permission. When the man nodded, the boy bounced out of his chair. Where was he getting his energy? He'd been ready to fold ten minutes earlier.

"So, ma'am," he asked from the depths of the icebox, "why do you keep your bread in the fridge?" He poked around in the refrigerator and dug out a jar of guava jam.

Curious little monkey. Definitely not from the area if he didn't know that. "Bugs," Sarah muttered.

"Bugs. Yeah, I suppose." His expression was sagely understanding, a pint-sized guru. The light shone on his thin wrists.

Didn't he get enough to eat? Sarah wondered. He seemed awfully small and stringy.

"So what kind of bugs?" By now he'd opened the jar and stuck his index finger in, unself-consciously tasting it.

The man had tipped his chair back against the counter and watched the proceedings through half-closed eyes as though he were running a tally sheet on her.

"The bugs, ma'am." The boy leaned against her hip, his face tipped to hers.

She moved sideways, away from him, before she could stop herself. His small bones against her were unbearable, like an accusation. Clearing her throat, she ignored his expression. "Cockroaches. Florida has huge cockroaches."

"Yeah?" He was enraptured. "Roaches! Really big, huh?"

"Well, sometimes we call them palmetto bugs because they nest in palmetto trees, but we have new bugs now, Asian cockroaches, bigger, meaner." She felt as if she were at the Mad Hatter's tea party. Midnight intruders. Cockroaches. She sliced the toast into rectangles and poured soup into a green bowl. "Here."

"So how big, a foot?" The plate and bowl dangled precariously from the boy's dirty fingers and his narrow face sparkled.

"Enough, Nicholas," a commanding voice broke in. "Eat." The man's chair banged on the floor. Sarah jumped. "Thank the lady."

"Yeah, right, but, Jake, I really want to know about them cockroaches. She don't mind, do you, ma'am?" Nicholas leaned against her again.

Sarah shook her head. "I don't mind." Her hand trembled.

"See, Jake? She don't mind about the bugs. She just don't want me leaning up on her. Probably because I'm so dirty. You told me not to roll down that hill." He swallowed a huge mouthful that had swollen his cheeks up like a chipmunk's.

She wanted to cry. The man's eyes were on her, a strange pity moving in them. She turned off the burner. "They're just big bugs, Nicholas. They fly."

The boy nodded, content.

Sarah gave the man soup and iced tea and poured 7-Up for Nicholas.

"I don't have any milk for your boy." She opened the icebox door and put the bread and jam inside. "Have more iced tea if you want," she said, setting the pitcher down with just enough force that it tilted forward, spilling the cold tea down the man's chest and thighs.

"What the hell?" He leaped to his feet. The plate skidded across the tea-splashed table.

Sarah whirled. She could make it out the back door. She could.

His muscular arm caught her around the middle.

"Oomph." The breath was knocked out of her. Looking into his annoyed eyes, she drew a deep breath. "Turn me loose, please."

"What?" He glanced down at his palm splayed across her middle, his square fingers tight against the tiny flowers of her shirt. "Sorry." He looked at his hand as if surprised by its quick movement.

"See, Jake? She don't like you touching her, neither. Even if you're not as dirty as me." The boy's bright blue gaze shifted between the two adults. His tone carried a note of satisfaction.

Sarah still felt the warm imprint of those muscles against her stomach.

"Jake, you and me need a bath." The boy's face was peaceful. Filled up with toast and soup, he sat there with a sleepy grin splitting his mud-flecked face, his teeth a white line drawn through the grime.

Sarah heard Jake's quiet breathing, heard her own heart beating in her ears. She smelled her own fear rising from her.

Nicholas laid his face sideways on the table and sleepily traced noodle circles on the plate. "That guava's good. Maybe sometime I can have it on toast."

Jake hadn't moved. Up close like this, Sarah saw a thread of gray in the glossy brown of his beard. His aggressiveness frightened her, but those light brown eyes didn't. They judged her, pitied her, dismissed her.

At her indrawn breath, he stepped back. "Look, I barged in here like a Brahma bull, I reckon." He was uncomfortable, as though he'd just realized how she'd taken his actions.

She stepped carefully back. "You did." Sarah sensed the easing of tension. Perhaps she'd overreacted. He really hadn't *done* anything. It was just his attitude. He was rude, crude, and probably tattooed, but he hadn't actually forced his way in.

"God knows what you must have thought." Once again his eyes watched her knowingly.

She saw Nicholas's lashes droop. "I think it's clear what I thought."

He glanced towards his son, whose sleepy snores disturbed the quiet. "Yeah, I can't blame you, I guess. But you must be used to all kinds of activity out here, day and night. People must drop in at night." Watching, watching.

What was he suggesting? Sarah turned back to the sink, washing the knife. "Not really."

"Don't you get a lot of people wanting to go night-fishing?" He moved around the boy, touching his neck lightly as he passed.

"No. People make arrangements ahead of time if they plan on using my boats at night." She swished the dishrag over the table, scrubbing hard at a splotch. Rinsing the rag out, she draped it over the sink and faced him.

She was tired of this cat-and-mouse game. Weary fatalism sapped her energy. Whatever was going to happen, would. Her sympathies were all with the mouse. No wonder it got pounced on. It didn't have the patience to outwait the cat. "Look, if you're trying to scare me, okay, you have. I don't know what game you're playing, but why are you here?"

"I told you. Nicholas got sick, probably because he's been in the car too long and he's tired. He's afraid of the dark around here. You know how kids are sometimes. They get the most ridiculous notions. Then I saw your sign."

"How?"

He hooked his thumbs in his belt. "From the road."

"It's a small sign with no lights."

He looked straight into her own eyes, almost as though he knew how nearsighted she was. "I have good eyesight."

"You must." Sarah tried to figure out why his simplest statements sounded like lies. Her fingers smoothed the wet dishrag. "I think it's time you and your son leave." Skirting the table, she cast a quick glance at the sleeping boy. He should be home in bed; not humped over a kitchen table at one o'clock in the morning.

"We can't." The man's voice was flat and low.

Her hands gripped the chair where the boy slept. "What do you mean, you can't?" Even in the chill air, sweat beaded her forehead. With an effort, she kept her voice down. "You have to!"

Suddenly he was at her side, his rough whisper matching her tone. "We can't. The truck has a flat."

"Fix it!" Sarah took two steps away from his rugged strength.

"I don't have a spare. I thought you might have one. This being a fishing camp, you must carry spare parts." He circled between her and the back door.

"Well, I don't." Sarah forced her words out. "You have to leave. I don't want you here."

"Yeah, you made that clear, all right. I can understand you not wanting to let us in at first, but you couldn't even spare a sick kid something to eat without having your arm twisted." Contempt colored his voice.

Put that way, her reluctance to let him and his son in seemed cheap and stingy, not cautious. But she didn't have to justify herself to him. *He* was the intruder. "Now just a minute—" As he leaned forward, his jeans brushed her bare thighs, sending a shiver over her skin. She pulled back. "You should have thought about that before dragging him out at this time of night." She smoothed her hair off her forehead and saw him follow the movements of her fingers down to her cutoffs. Suddenly she didn't know what to do with her hands.

The hum of the ice-maker was followed by the thunking of cubes into the tray. The anger faded from his eyes. "Yeah, you're right," he said tiredly, "I should have thought about a lot of things. But I didn't." He looked back at his son for a long moment. "We can't leave tonight."

Sarah looked at the grimy scrap with his thin fingers smeared with God-knew-what-kind of dirt and smashed noodles. She really didn't want this pitiful child in her home. His wiry energy and intelligence tugged at her memories. She wanted him gone. "I don't rent cabins. You can't stay here."

"Hell. You have a big house. Can't you find a corner somewhere? I mean, I don't want to inconvenience you or anything." Sarcasm lashed his rough voice. "You're a real sweetheart, you are. Haven't you ever heard the story about the Good Samaritan?"

Her skin flushed with a temper she rarely let loose anymore, but she was tired and confused and the boy had rubbed against old pain, leaving her off balance. "Look, this isn't my problem. You're the one who took off in the middle of the night with your son. You're the one who didn't plan ahead. Don't take out your guilt on me!"

A cabbage palm branch rattled against the roof, broken loose by the rising wind. Jake inhaled deeply. Sarah saw the visible effort he made to defuse the tension as he spoke. "I fouled up. But I need help now." He paused. His voice was expressionless when he continued. "For the kid."

Sarah felt petulant and didn't much like herself at the moment. Her hand strayed to touch the back of the boy's washed-to-no-color shirt. She stopped the inadvertent movement. They could sleep on the porch. No, she thought, as she saw the man's judgmental eyes, that won't do.

A sniffle escaped from the child. He needed a bed and he'd been ill. She could let him sleep upstairs. "All right." She rubbed her arms. "Do you want to carry him or wake him so he can walk up?" She wasn't experienced with kids. She didn't know which would be better, but she hated to ruin his sleep.

The man's decisiveness irritated her. "I'll carry him. Unless, of course," his tone was snide, "you want me to wake him up and give him a bath?"

The ache in her throat stopped her retort. Had she really seemed so nasty? "Carry him, then. Bedroom on the left of the stairs, but you sleep outside in your truck."

"Whatever you say." Carefully the man lifted his son out of the chair and tucked the small head under his bearded chin. The boy sighed and flung out an arm. The man placed it carefully on the boy's thin chest. "Why don't you lead the way?" His gaze mocked her. "That way you can make sure we don't nab the family silver."

She didn't want to go up the stairs with him. Every cell in her body buzzed with alarm. Even with his arms filled with his son, even now that he'd clarified his presence, he made her uneasy. His unconcealed contempt made her uncomfortable. She wasn't used to other people analyzing her actions and finding them lacking. Her own judgment? That was a horse of a different color. She'd grown used to living with her inadequacies. Her conscience was harder on her than any pale-eyed stranger could ever be. He hadn't earned the right to judge her.

"You know, mister, you're awfully rude to someone who's let you in, fed you and your son, and is now giving him a bed for the night. Haven't *you* heard the story about biting the hand that feeds you?" Healthy anger chased out her disquiet. She led the way, feeling him close behind her the whole way up the long staircase with its wide, shallow steps.

Jake resisted a cheap comeback, but he bared his teeth. She wasn't what he'd expected. He watched the smooth curves of her thighs and ankles as she walked up the stairs. She had the tiniest waist and most beautiful bottom it had been his pleasure to see in years.

He'd been angry before she even opened the door. Driving around for hours trying to make up his mind whether to stop at her place or not. And then Nicholas had gotten sick. He'd taken too long to decide and then, when he had, he wanted in. Her caution had ticked him off. Once there, he wanted to settle the score with her. Get it over with.

When she opened the door, he'd been knocked back in his shoes. Her wide, dark blue gaze staring blindly at him, her small face carefully checking him out, her hand brandishing that damn bat had plunged him into a fury. Her silky smooth hair the color of wet leaves in autumn made his fingers twitch with a need to stroke its smoothness, to see if it felt as soft as it looked. He'd wanted to touch the slim neck where a vein pulsed with fear. Anger and something else, something dark and primitive, had stirred in him at the sight of her.

He'd wanted to crack that ridiculous bat in two.

Nicholas stirred. Poor kid. She was right. He shouldn't have kept the kid out so late, but Jake's own devilish temper had whipped at his shoulders, telling him to stop, to deal with her. Finally he'd given in. As he'd coasted to a stop under the trees, he'd leaned on the steering wheel and known he was making a mistake. Nicholas had scooted over to the door and said wearily, "We getting out now, Jake? 'Cause I don't feel so good."

When Jake slashed the truck tire, Nicholas looked at him and they both stooped, listening to the hiss of air as the tire flattened into the sand. Jake hadn't explained. "Come on, Nicholas," he'd said and strode to the screen door showing in the dim, yellow light cast by a mosquito bulb over the frame.

And that had been that.

Now, her eyes wary, she paused before the door of a cool, dark room with twin beds. "Go ahead." Her reluctance to have him in her house fueled his desire to be there, to stay there, to see the look on her face when it was all over with. She wasn't going to get rid of him.

He slid Nicholas between sheets smelling of apples and roses, gratified by the smear of dirt the boy put across the immaculate blue surface. Would she flinch at that the way she had when the kid leaned against her? Let her.

Jake straightened and bumped into her. She'd followed him in, after all. She was looking at Nicholas. Probably wondering how she was going to sanitize her sheets. He smiled vindictively and thought about crawling between those same clean sheets in his own dirt. He glanced at her.

She was still watching the boy, her back straight as an arrow, chin up.

Her breasts moved once with a deep breath, a small movement that disturbed him. He wished he knew what she was thinking. The loose, flowered shirt fell just past her waist, the bottom button gaping an inch or so above the band of her shorts. A tiny freckle beckoned from the gap.

Nicholas flipped over, twisting the sheet with him.

She turned away. "There you are, then. I'll shut the door behind me." She walked away, closing him out again.

He snagged the edge of her sleeve, touched the goose bumps on her arm. "Wait."

Shadows tinted the skin under her eyes. "Yes?"

"I'm going to take a bath." He wouldn't ask her permission.

She nodded. "All right." Some spark had drained from her. He missed it. He followed the narrow lines of her back down the long hall runner that muffled their steps. The hour and the strangeness isolated them, magnified every breath, every look. Her glance thrown back over her shoulder assumed an importance he didn't think she intended. In the shadowy hall, she lured him forward, a reed in the stream beckoning deeper to the secret depths. He felt entangled in secrets as she whispered to him in the silence and shadows.

"There's the bathroom. You can find towels underneath the sink."

Checking out the bathroom, Jake leaned over her shoulder just as she backed out of his way. Her bare heels bumped the hard toes of his boots. He reached out to steady her, but she'd already turned and his palms met warm arms, delicate bones, soft woman. He wanted to keep his hands there, on her warmth and softness. He wanted to move her exquisite bones over him. When he saw the shock in her eyes, he dropped his hands. She wasn't going to get an apology. He wasn't the least bit sorry.

"I have to go out to the truck for my stuff. Okay?"

She shrugged, the cotton moving over her skin in soft sibilance. The sound was loud in his ears, calling to mind skin and sheets and all the things he didn't want to think of.

Grabbing his bag from the pickup, he hurried back to the old house with its dark windows. Standing on the front stoop, he paused for a moment to savor the damp air and night sounds. Way off in the distance he heard a boat engine chugging up from the canal to the lake.

A sense of finality flooded him. He'd started a chain of events whose end he couldn't see.

Sarah waited for the bang of the screen door before she moved. She didn't want to encourage that look that changed his eyes into golden cat eyes. Better to stay out of his way. The boy whimpered in distress. Sarah rubbed the newel post, back and forth. He whimpered again, and she moved quietly down the hall to his room.

He was tangled in his sheets. Half asleep, he couldn't fight his way free. From her own childhood, she remembered the fright. Behind her, she heard the man close the bathroom door and turn on the shower.

"Shh, Nicholas. I'll untangle you. Hold still." Sarah touched his forehead, smoothed the dirt-stiffened hair off his face, traced the stubborn chin. Carefully she untwisted the sheet, lifting his surprising weight and trying not to wake him completely. She slipped his socks off and reached into the chifforobe near the bed for a light blanket which she tucked around him.

"Hi, ma'am." His sleepy smile caught her unawares, and she smiled back at him.

"Hi, yourself." She pulled the blanket up closer to his chin.

"Is it day, yet?"

"No, not for a long time. Just sleep, okay? Your father's taking a shower. He'll be here in a minute."

"You make him take a bath?" The boy yawned and rolled away from her as he said in a sleep-muted voice, "But he's

not my dad. Silly Jake, cutting the tire . . ." A deep breath
and he sank back into sleep.

Sarah sat on the edge of the bed. She didn't hear the
shower. The upstairs phone was in the hall, just past the
bathroom. As she stood up, the bedsprings rattled.

She had to get to the phone. Passing the bathroom, she
saw the light under the door, heard him moving on the
linoleum floor. Had he heard her? She froze. The door
stayed closed.

She inched her way to the phone and picked it up. For a
moment she couldn't remember the police number, and then
when she did, her fingers were trembling so hard she
couldn't dial. She was dizzy with fear.

Suddenly water dripped onto her arm. A big, wet hand
unwrapped her fingers from the phone. She turned and saw
first the ropy chest muscles, the thick chest hair moving
down to unsnapped jeans. Reaching for the phone, her hand
slipped and slid down the still wet muscles, sleek and hard,
to his jeans.

He'd shaved his beard off. Released from the shaggy
beard and moustache, a face craggy with angles and cheekbones stared at her and he said very gently, returning the
phone to its cradle, "You don't want to make that phone
call."

Chapter Two

Sarah's fingers were wet where he'd gripped them. As he placed the receiver back down, she wiped her hands dry on the front of her shirt. He was absolutely still, but the knowledge of violence controlled by a powerful will crackled between them. Like waves rolling in steadily, building power before the immense ninth wave that drives everything before it, his restraint beat at her skin, pressed on her pores, rolled over her.

"Who are you?" she breathed.

He didn't answer. His breath sighed onto her. On his neck a bead of blood welled up through a bit of toilet paper. He peeled the paper off, looked at it as if not sure how it came to be there and wadded it between his thumb and forefinger absentmindedly as he considered her. His warm, wet hand pressed hers down onto the receiver, cutting off the buzzing of the earpiece. Sarah shivered.

His light brown eyes, more startling than ever without the distraction of his heavy beard, were cold again. A speck of shaving cream showed in the cleft of a square chin. He'd hurried, then, nicking himself in his haste, drying his face carelessly. In a dark, wet strip, his chest hair carved a line down his muscles, separating them, emphasizing their strength, before disappearing below his navel in an ever-narrowing path. He ran his hand over his chest, drying it. Water dotted the floor. Sarah wondered if it would leave white spots that she'd have to polish out tomorrow. The possibility of such a homey action seemed far away.

"Please," she whispered again. "Who are you? Why are you here?"

"Look," he ran his hand once more over the curling hair of his chest, a drop of water flicking in her direction where she felt its damp coolness on her breast. "This is ridiculous."

She almost reached up to rub the wet spot dry, but she was afraid to move. Its chill burned her skin. Could she grab the telephone and smash him? No, she wouldn't look at the phone. Wouldn't even think of it. Her eyelid twitched with strain.

He sighed again and moved her carefully away from the phone. She'd given herself away somehow. His palm and fingers were hot on her arm where they curled together, meeting just under the sleeve. It was an intimate touch. A shudder rose up from her toes.

His finger rubbed the inner skin of her arm. "Look, can we talk?"

The banality of his statement made Sarah giddy with fear and relief. A warm, clean smell of soap drifted to her nose. Her soap, exotic and scented with musk, on his skin.

Suddenly she realized how close they were. His jeans scratched her knees. The metal belt buckle hanging loose from the jeans was a cold stroke on her inner thigh. She felt the prick of the tab against her skin.

With its sharp touch, something dangerous and unexpected crept into the quiet. His breathing quickened and his hand slid higher on her arm. A floorboard creaked with his restless movement.

His bare instep brushed against the outside of her foot and in the opening of her shirt his chest hair grazed her skin. A quiver rippled through her stomach. He felt the ripple. His face told her so. So, too, did the slow stroke up and down her captured arm.

She pulled against his fingers, lifting them with all her strength. Momentarily they tightened, then freed her. Only now did her heart speed erratically, a sickening rhythm of fear and excitement.

Sarah whirled, her heart pumping madly for flight.

"God, what a mess. Wait." His large arm once more wrapped around her, efficiently halting her.

Her heels stung from the skidding slide on the hall rug.

She almost stuttered in her frenzy to speak. "Just go, go. I swear I won't tell anyone you were here. Leave the boy—" Ah no, she thought as his hand tightened on her. He'd kidnapped the boy. "Just go, please." She tried not to sob.

"Easy, look, I'm not touching you. Just hold still a minute and listen to me, okay?" He raised his hands palms up to her.

Sarah swayed, but he didn't touch her. She gripped her hands tightly to stop their shaking. "I'm listening." She couldn't hear anything except his harsh breathing. "I won't run," she added as he moved closer to her. His exasperated expression calmed her by its very ordinariness. "But you're right," she said. "This is ridiculous. You can't stop me from making a phone call." She poked her trembling hands into the pockets of her shorts, pulling the threads at the bottom. If she could keep him talking, distract him . . . "You came shoving your way in here—"

"Now wait just a minute! I didn't *shove* my way in anywhere! And I didn't force your door open. Although with those flimsy locks I could have and, believe me, it would have been faster than waiting for you to decide whether or not you wanted to let some sick kid into your house. Here," he dug deep into the pocket of his jeans, "here's a quarter." He flung the coin towards her. "Isn't that about the going rate for a public bathroom?"

The coin rattled on the floor. Sarah gasped.

Jake frowned. "Hell." Holding her still, he stooped to pick up the coin. He'd really screwed it up. Why had he grabbed the phone from her like that? Of course he'd scared her. But something nasty in his nature had wanted to scare her, mess up her pretty sheets, push against her. What a pig he was. He should have defused the situation, not poured kerosene on it.

When he'd seen her with the receiver at her ear, though, he'd known she was calling the police. He couldn't afford that. He should have reacted differently, but her softness and vulnerability triggered something in him he couldn't curb. If all that softness and smoothness and that tender blue stare hadn't knocked him for a loop when she first opened the door, he'd have been fine. He just had to kill this leap in his blood when he was around her. Staying angry wasn't the way. Anger could slide too easily into something else. He'd just had proof of that.

Why in hell had he flung the quarter at her like that, though? He rubbed the cleft of his chin and looked at the bit of shaving cream. Good thing he'd hurried. Hell to pay if the police had roared in. No, he couldn't have police showing up.

Holding the coin in his hand, Jake flipped it up and down while he thought. Heads. Tails. Heads. He flipped the coin one last time and held it in his fingers, turning it in the dim light. "I'm sorry I scared you." He handed her the coin.

Her fingers were icy as he folded them around the quarter, and he wanted to kick himself for being so cynical. "Can we go downstairs? This whole situation has gone cockeyed. I'm not going to hurt you," he insisted. "Believe me, if I were going to do anything, I'd have already done it.''

Sarah believed him. His voice rang with conviction. Thinking about his actions, she had to admit to herself that he'd been careful not to hurt her, but his very presence threatened her. ''I guess so,'' she admitted, still uneasy.

Making up her mind, she slipped the coin into her pocket. Whatever he was up to, this hostile-eyed male wasn't going to attack her.

How she'd reached that decision, she wasn't sure. Maybe the way he'd waited for her to say something. Maybe the fact that he'd never really threatened her. Or maybe it was the way he treated his son. No, that *was* the problem. She rubbed the edges of the coin. The boy wasn't his son. That was why she'd scurried to the phone. She'd thought the boy was kidnapped. And the tires. That was what had frightened her out of her wits. The premeditation and violence.

When she'd seen the man's face, though, the situation had subtly changed. The rugged nakedness of his face had been angry but controlled. He'd been tense, intimidating but not violent.

Sarah motioned him down the stairs first. ''Okay, we'll talk in the kitchen, but this whole situation doesn't make sense. Your actions don't add up. You arrive on my doorstep in the middle of the night, scare me to death, and—and you're rude!'' She was talking too fast as adrenaline flooded her blood. ''I'll listen, but ante up quick.''

She relished the pop-pop-popping of rage in her. Oh, she was in a fine rage. She'd been such a mope, letting this thick-necked, thick-headed stranger push her around, take over, scare her witless. She'd decided a long time ago no one would ever treat her like that again, and still she'd almost fallen into the trap.

It was the night, the hour. That was all. Anybody would be muddled, and the sweet melancholy of the dream hadn't helped. ''Sit.'' She yanked out a chair but didn't push him into it. Her rage wasn't that foolhardy. His face was void of all expression. Was he laughing at her? She scowled. He'd better not. She'd brain him with a skillet if he laughed. "Talk."

Jake knew he was going to have to make it good. A quick, sideways glance showed him that pulse beating frantically at the side of her neck. Near panic, she'd doubt everything he said. What had sent her running to the phone? Had Nicholas let something slip?

Her lips were slightly pursed. Even tightened with anger, her bottom lip glowed, a soft pink fullness. He couldn't help noticing that softness. Didn't want to. He spread his hands flat on the table. "Ante up, huh? From where I sit, you hold all the cards." She blinked. Good. He'd surprised her.

"*I* do?" She narrowed her eyes in what he figured was speculation. Then her eyes strayed to his chest. Stayed there for a long moment.

He shrugged. "Sure you do." His chest warmed where her eyes lingered. "Look, can I put on my shirt before we finish this conversation?" Rising, he leaned over the table. "I think we'd both be more comfortable." He was feeling hostile again. It was those damned soft eyes looking at him, touching him with their nearsighted blue velvet.

"Oh. Of course. Yes." Her face was now as pink as her bottom lip.

He took his time getting a shirt from the bag he'd brought in earlier, thinking hard. What would she buy? Better to stick with the truth, as far as possible. Truth always sounded more credible. What were the weak spots in his story? The time, of course. The place itself. Why would he be in the Okeechobee area? Possibly visiting the Seminole reservation?

He rubbed his chin. Scraping off that damned beard had felt good. He should have done that as soon as he had got back in the country. He buttoned the last button as he reentered the kitchen.

She hadn't moved, but her expression had changed. She must have thought of some more questions. Hell. This might be a long, drawn out situation, and he couldn't lay any booby traps for himself farther up the trail. He folded himself into a chair.

Her husky voice confronted him. "Okay. I want to know about the tires."

Sheesh. Jake decided she was either very shrewd or naive. He had to admire her courage, though, in going right for the kill. "They're flat. I told you." He shielded his expression.

She sat up straighter. "You're lying."

"Now why on earth would I lie about something like that?" He smiled.

She rubbed her eyes tiredly. "I don't know. Nicholas said you cut the tires on your truck."

"Is that what this is all about? Nicholas said I cut the tires?" Jake laughed casually. "Kids. He saw me work out the spike I'd run over. Anyway, that's easy to check," he said, half rising. "Want to take a look? I'll wait here while you see for yourself." Her hesitancy amused him. She'd never make a poker player. "No?" He sank back into the kitchen chair.

"You lied about Nicholas," she persisted. "Nicholas said you're not his father."

"I never lied. I just said he was my boy." Jake frowned.

"You know what the phrase implies. You know what I thought." She concentrated her attention on him. Slicking a strand of autumn brown hair behind her ear, she continued, "So why lie—pardon me, *imply*, that he was your son if you didn't have something to hide?"

Buying time, Jake stretched out his legs, bumping her feet. There was the rub, of course. He did have something to hide. And he knew she had her own secrets. "Nicholas wasn't well, I didn't feel like going into a long explanation and I figured anybody running a fishing camp would be glad to help out. How was I to know you were here alone?'' Half-truth.

''But at midnight?'' She wrinkled her nose.

Jake shifted in his seat. ''Yeah, well, look, this is embarrassing. I got lost. We were headed towards Moore Haven and stopped off at the reservation, wandered around a while and I guess I got off the main drag.'' Was he overplaying it?

She rubbed her nose. The action was childlike and oddly appealing.

Jake crossed his ankles, his toes brushing hers under the table. They were small, cold, the way her fingers had been when he put the quarter in them. ''I don't know this area. I got lost. No street signs.''

She nodded slowly. ''A lot of people get lost down here.'' She thought it through. ''But what on earth possessed you to keep the boy out so late?'' She was straightening with suspicion.

''You know how it is with kids.'' His words brought vertical white lines around her mouth. ''One thing leads to another. It got late, dark. I didn't know where I was.''

She frowned as she folded her hands in front of her on the table. The small ovals of her nails were glossy. ''You look as though you always know where you are.''

Damn. ''Yeah? Usually I do. The Glades are different, though, aren't they?''

She nodded again. Then she returned to the original subject. ''The boy's not your son?''

He shook his head.

''Who is he, then? What's he doing with you?''

And wouldn't he just love to tell her? Wouldn't that frost her punkins? ''His dad was a friend of mine.'' The less he said, the better. Watch out, Donnelly, or your rear'll be out on the porch so fast your face'll be left behind.

''*Was*?'' Her brows met in thought.

He'd interested her. Jake observed her closely. "He died recently. I wanted to get the boy away from everything. Give him a change of scenery."

"What about his mother? Why would she let him go off with you? Why wouldn't she want him with her, especially now? The boy must be grieving for his father. Surely this isn't the time to upset his routine? Why would his mother let you take him?" Her questions tumbled from lips gone white.

Interesting that she should be so intense. "Whoa. One thing at a time." Jake looked around the kitchen. "Could I impose for a cup of coffee? Anything?"

Her frown was scornful. "I don't think it will hurt you to wait, okay? Let's get the questions answered first."

"Cautious little thing, aren't you? Not that I blame you." He scratched his chin. "How about a glass of water? Or is that too much trouble?" Deliberately he made his tone derisive.

"Don't be unpleasant. It is, actually, under the circumstances, but all right. And another thing," she glared at him over her shoulder as she ran the faucet full blast, "don't patronize me by calling me a 'little thing,' okay?" Water slopped onto the floor as she slammed the glass in front of him.

He sipped. Brackish, like the lake.

"I'm waiting." Water had splashed down the front of her blouse and through wet white spots skin glistened pink and shadowy.

"Okay, I'm responsible for him right now. His mother wasn't available."

"You're still lying." She stood up hastily.

Oh, hell. Jake rubbed his head hard. "Look, that's the third time you've said that. Don't accuse me of lying again unless you're ready to put your money where your mouth is." He glanced irritably at her pink lips. "And sit down, will you? You make me nervous jumping around like a scalded cat. It's the truth. The boy needed to get away from the situation he was in. I helped out. That's all there is to it, no big deal.''

Her fingers rubbed the wet cotton, lifting it away from her skin. "You're leaving something out."

Jake drained the glass of water and banged it down. "Of course I am! Who are you to think you have the right to know this kid's personal tragedies, huh? I asked you for simple human kindness, and you're taking on like a mystery dropped in your lap! Helping out doesn't buy you the kid's history, understand? He's got a right to privacy."

He planted his fists on the table and leaned over her, forcing her to look up at him. "Doesn't he?"

He'd embarrassed her with the accusation of nosiness, but she blazed ahead. "You haven't answered my question, you know," she reminded him anxiously. "You're not being straightforward with me."

Damn right he wasn't. Damn right he wasn't going to answer all her clever little questions.

"I may not have the right to intrude on a private tragedy, but you've intruded on me and I want some assurance that you have the right to this child." She tapped one finger on the table. "I don't believe you'd hurt me, but I'm not satisfied with your explanations."

"Look," he sighed, "I've been as straight as I can be. I don't know what you want me to say. I'm tired, hungry—in spite of that wonderfully generous sandwich of yours," he added with evident sarcasm. "What I want is to curl up somewhere and sleep for a week. If it'll make you feel better and calm your tidy little—sorry—soul, I'll sleep out in the pickup. I don't give a rat's good damn where I sleep right now, if you take my meaning!" He shoved the chair under the table. "You do what you want, but I'm crashing somewhere in five seconds flat."

At his vehemence, she made a small, troubled sound. He'd done the best he could. That was that, cards on the table, face up. Well, not completely face up, but it was showdown time for sure. Jake stomped towards the door.

"Wait!"

His bluff had worked.

"You'll need your boots." With a casual wave, she motioned upstairs. A gleam of mischief deepened the blue of her eyes.

So it hadn't worked. He'd overplayed it. "Yeah," he growled, taking the stairs two at a time. So he'd sleep in the truck. She'd made that clear earlier. He hadn't lost any ground, and it could've worked out worse. He didn't think she was going to call the police now. And for some reason, she'd decided to drop the questioning.

Too bad he hadn't been able to lull her doubts, though. He'd give a new dollar bill to know where he'd gone wrong.

Sitting on the bottom step he tugged on his boots. The pickup wasn't going to be comfortable. He stomped towards the door again, her muted laugh following him into the dark.

Jake draped as much of himself on the front seat as he could and then stuck the leftovers out the window. He was going to be paralyzed in the morning. He was much too old for these shenanigans. He'd really landed in the manure this time, damn it. Folding his arms over his chest, he sighed and went to sleep, the sound of voices on the lake floating in to him.

Sarah watched his tall form yank open the pickup door and slouch inside. She almost called him back. He was going to be cold, uncomfortable. Maybe she should have let him sleep inside, after all, but she hadn't pinned down that false note in his story. It was too late, though, and she was too tired to think about it anymore. Calling her a "little thing." He was lucky she hadn't poured the water on his head.

He poked his boots out the window towards her. Nothing subtle about that. Well, let him vent his temper in the cool air. It would do him good to know he couldn't push her around. How could he possibly think she would accept his comment that the boy's mother would let him go off after his father's death? The man was hiding something in spite of his foxy candor. Let him. His secrets didn't concern her.

Sarah locked the screen door again, noticing that the lock tongue was loose. She turned the knob hard, double-checking that the lock still held, and went inside.

As she closed the front door she looked back. A coot trilled its loneliness out on the lake. No moon and a chill wind. Not a good night to be outside, but Jake seemed tough.

Would the boy be frightened if he woke up alone? Sarah nibbled her thumb. She'd sleep downstairs. It was almost morning, and sleep had already escaped her for most of the night. If the boy woke up and wandered downstairs, she'd be there.

She walked silently upstairs and removed her pillow from her bed. A yawn stretched her throat. Maybe she would sleep, after all. She stuck her head into the boy's room. Not his room. Hers, she reminded herself, and would be hers again this time tomorrow.

Nicholas was all over the bedsheets, one foot dangling off the bed. His mouth was parted and a sigh bubbled out. One grimy fist twisted in the sheets. Sarah covered him with the blanket, her fingers lingering on the soft skin of his cheek. She knew she wouldn't feel safe until the boy and man left her home.

Back downstairs she wrapped herself again in the afghan and lay in the dark, thinking. She must have been mad to let them into her house. Moon mad, but there was no moon. What a strange night.

Even stranger was her reaction to Jake What's-his-name. Without a beard, his rough, dented face was powerfully sensual. The hard planes and angles were pure, primitive male, the kind of maleness that demanded its female complement, softness and surrender, the kind of maleness that

kept her uneasiness at a full boil. She burrowed into the
pillow and watched the shadows drift across the ceiling of
the old house.

In the morning, harsh bird cries and Nicholas's voice
calling woke Jake up. He'd slept, after all. Not a surprise
since he was used to interrupted sleep and rough lay-downs.
This one hadn't been the worst. In the cool night air sounds
from the lake had infiltrated his sleep and mingled with
dreams of Mexico and hot sun, beaches filled with bikini-
clad blondes. Then, in the dream, soft blue eyes wove in and
out of a blue, blue sea that swelled around him in an endless rocking.

A husky voice quieted Nicholas momentarily, but then the
screen door whomped, and Nicholas's pointed little face,
clean and scrubbed, peered in at him over the truck window rim. So she hadn't let the chance to tidy Nicholas escape her.

"Where'd you go, Jake? Why'd you sleep out here? You
look funny without a beard, Jake. You gonna grow it again?
I liked your beard. She," he tilted his chin to the house,
"make you shave it?"

"Slow down, shortcake. Old Jake's still booting up his
brain. Give me a sec."

"Sure, Jake, no problem. Listen, this is a great place. The
lady, she said I could call her Sarah, Jake, made me oatmeal. You ever heard of anybody putting ice cream on oatmeal? That's what she did, Jake. It's the truth." Nicholas
bounced up and down on the running board of the beat-up
truck, bouncing it back and forth.

"Enough, Nicholas." Jake plunked his feet on the floorboard and groaned. He was much too old for this. Even his
butt ached.

"Sure, Jake, but c'mon, I got something to show you."
Nicholas leaped off the truck, arms flying, tumbling into the
gray sand.

Life wasn't fair. All that energy shouldn't be packaged in one tiny frame. Should be spread around to people who needed it, like thirty-eight-year-old men who slept in trucks. Jake shoved open the door. Ahead, Nicholas, his arms extended into guns and his mouth screwed up so he could make "fpffpfffpt" sounds with his lips, dodged between trees and bushes. Jake didn't like this guerilla warfare game, but he wasn't going to stop it. First time Nicholas had run around much since they'd left.

"Wait, Nicholas." Jake grabbed Nicholas's shirt, dragging him to a halt. "What time did you get up, sport?"

"Early, I think." Nicholas kicked a Spanish moss clump until it shredded. "Wasn't dark, though."

"Good," Jake said grimly. Wonder what she'd thought when the dynamo came rolling downstairs? Come to think of it, how come Nicholas was in clean jeans and shirt? "What miracle happened overnight, kid? You look real spiffy." Jake tickled Nicholas's ear.

"She—Sarah—I mean, made me clean up. That's why I figured she made you shave your beard. I don't want to hurt your feelings, but it was getting smelly, Jake. You know what she did? While she was washing my stuff, she made me wear one of her shirts! Boy, am I glad none of the guys saw that! Yuck. They'd a called me a damned sissy girl."

"Not nice, Nicholas. All girls aren't sissies. Guys are squeamish even if they don't show it. And no more swearing."

"But that's what you always say, Jake. 'Damn fool this, damn fool that.'"

"Don't repeat everything you hear me say, kid, understand?"

"Well, the guys woulda made fun. You know that, Jake. They'd a laughed their heads off, me in a girl's shirt! Double yuck!" Nicholas sprinted ahead and threw himself into a wood-slatted swing dangling lopsidedly from a live oak tree.

Curling onto the ground, Spanish moss dripped in long swaths from the tree branches. Belly down, he swung in crazy loops over the hollowed-out ground beneath him.

The swing had been there for years. The whole place had that look of permanence. Jake hadn't seen such a *permanent* look to a house in years. Off toward the lake he could see a dock and several motorboats. Not much of an operation. Those boats looked too small for the motor he'd heard last night when he arrived. Could she be involved in something illegal out here? He looked around. Perfect setup if she were, and it would fit what he knew about her.

He knocked on the screen door before opening it. That ought to shock her out of her socks.

The sight of her almost shocked *him* out of *his* socks. Her small, heart-shaped rear end was all he saw at first. Then he realized that she was kneeling on the floor near the couch with her cheek slanted awkwardly on one arm while the other arm swung back and forth under the couch. Her shiny purple blouse hung loose, and he had a mouth-drying glimpse of that freckle on her stomach, and farther up soft curves in some barely there flesh-colored silk. At least he hoped it was silk. Hell of a wasted fantasy if it weren't.

"Oh." She scrambled up awkwardly. "I thought you were Nicholas."

She blushed, but he liked the way she didn't pretend she hadn't seen his reaction and heard his deep breath. She wasn't coy. No, she was direct. Maybe she'd be just as direct in bed—but he knew secrets stirred within her soft body, secrets he could hate her for, so he wasn't going to let himself find out.

"I was trying to get the bat for Nicholas." Her hands dropped helplessly to her sides and her expression was embarrassed, vulnerable.

"He's not far behind." Jake cleared his throat.

She wiped her hands down the sides of her black jeans, and he inhaled again as she lifted her hands to her hair where a cobweb clung. Her breasts moved upwards with her arms and she was his night dream, beckoning, drawing him to her. He stepped forward, drawn in spite of himself to the promise of her softness.

"Jake? Look what I got!" The screen door slammed behind Nicholas's pell-mell entrance. His face looked as though he'd tried to shovel the yard with it and in his hands he cupped a tiny, emerald frog. "Look at 'im! He's a wonder, huh, Jake? Huh, Sarah?"

Sarah pressed her cool hands against her flaming cheeks as she turned to Nicholas. Stepping forward, she tucked her blouse in her waistband. She knew what had swum through Jake's eyes. That slight flare of his nostrils had set off some inner trembling in her. She wasn't used to that kind of out-and-out, unashamed wanting. She'd never felt it herself but, oh, she recognized it on his face. That look twisted at her, deep, deep. She hurt to think about the way his gaze had moved over her, touching her in places no longer touched.

His expression clearly said he didn't give a damn that she'd seen his need. His refusal to back off, to deny what he'd felt, had set her heart beating erratically and stolen her breath. She swallowed. "Nicholas, he's a wonderful frog."

The boy moved carefully toward her, and she sensed Jake staring at her. When she looked up, flustered in spite of herself, Jake's eyes had turned hard, cold, hostile. Her hair slid over her cheek as she looked down at Nicholas's prize. "May I see?" She crouched down to eye level. Unblinking, the frog watched her. Sarah touched its tiny, squat body delicately.

"You're not a sissy! Jake was right. Mostly he is, you know." Nicholas stroked the frog's flat head.

Sarah spared Jake a quick glance. He was looking again at Nicholas, and a grin creased Jake's face, lightening the clear brown eyes that had darkened on her.

"Just remember that the next time, sport." Jake stepped in back of Nicholas.

Now Jake could watch her, watch the way her slim, brown hand moved next to Nicholas's as she touched the damp, green frog. She didn't mind touching the little creature, but she sure hadn't wanted Nicholas and his dirt near her.

That reaction underscored Jake's feelings about her, made him want to stay a country mile away from the seduction of her skin and eyes and softness. He had to remember she was tough and calculating.

He couldn't ever let himself forget coldness in the sweet scent and feel of her. He had to solve this situation and get out quickly before it was too late. Then her face lifted to him, her eyes an unfocused blue. He hooked his thumbs under his armpits, felt the tingle of her all over his skin.

Jake looked away. "Nicholas, you can't keep him."

"No, Jake?" The bony little body slumped in disappointment.

"Right, Ms.—?" Jake waited for her to identify herself, wondering why he was compelled to push at her. He wanted her to trip herself up, but he should just confront her, do the deed and go on down the road. Nobody had told him how he had to wrap things up. He could do it now, now in the morning sunshine, here in this shabby, cozy living room marked by years of living, he could do it, he could, he could. And walk away.

Her back turned to him, she answered, "Simpson. Sarah Jane Simpson."

So she'd kept her maiden name. Bitterness ate at him.

He crowded her, stuck a hand in her direction. "Jake Donnelly." Her hand was cool in his, slightly rough from outdoor work. He didn't dare underestimate her. He had to remember those calluses, remember that she was tougher than she looked. She'd earned those visible calluses as well as others, less visible.

"Yes, well, Mr. Donnelly, you can use my phone to make arrangements to fix your truck and then you can get on wherever you were going." She led him to the phone.

"That may be a problem, Ms. Simpson."

"Don't let it be." She swung open the kitchen door.

Her damned cool, lady-of-the-manor dismissal was eating away at his control, just the way her refusal to let him and Nicholas in last night had made him frighten her just a little. He hadn't been completely honest with her about not forcing his way in. But he hadn't been completely honest about much with her. Oh, sure, he hadn't physically broken down her door, though he'd wanted to for a mad instant when he thought she wasn't going to let Nicholas in. But in his need to see those eyes a little frightened, Jake had deliberately intimidated her. It wasn't nice of him, but then he'd never been a nice guy. Being nice wasn't his stock in trade.

Sarah led him to the kitchen, hating to walk in front of him. She didn't like the way he looked at her, as though he were figuring something out. Jake still made her very nervous. He looked like a man on the edge. She'd seen men like that in the Glades. There were stories circulating about men who'd reached that line that kept them on the side of civilization and then crossed over into the wild. She didn't care what drove Jake Donnelly and the boy wasn't her concern.

She wouldn't think about the child. He hadn't been kidnapped, and he wasn't being abused. Whoever Jake was, whatever he was, his actions showed that he cared for the boy. So, too, did his face when it softened as he looked at Nicholas. Sarah handed Jake the phone. "There. Make your arrangements—and quickly, please."

He shut the door of the kitchen behind him, closing her in with him, his wide shoulders between her and the door. He hooked the receiver on her shoulder, his muscular forearm lying against her breast. She didn't like what stirred in the shallows of his brown eyes.

Jake wanted to rip at her composure. The need to do so itched at him and made him wonder what she'd do if he moved his elbow over the delicate nipple that lay under his arm. He could feel its small heat clear to his bones, down to his groin. His damnable temper spurred him on, urged him to move in on her, disturb her. Under his arm her heart beat steadily on, a puny engine throbbing against the oncoming tide, and her eyes widened under his.

Chapter Three

Sarah saw hard muscles, warm male, and a look in Jake's eyes that she wouldn't tolerate. "Move your hand. I don't like these little games you're playing." Her cousins had loved to intimidate her when she was a kid. She'd spent some time figuring out how to make them back off, and when she had, they'd never terrorized her again.

Jake wasn't her cousin, though. He didn't move that arm that lay on her, a heavy, hot weight. His thumb nudged just under the notched lapel of her purple blouse. She felt it steal against her collar bone. Raising her chin, pushing against him with the force of her will, she repeated, "I told you to move your hand. I meant it."

Jake wondered what she'd do if he moved his whole body on her, took those soft lips tight now with anger under his. The look in her blazing eyes told him he'd be walking with a limp and talking like a soprano if he tried. She didn't realize how her face telegraphed her thoughts to someone like him. She was outgunned and still wouldn't give an inch. Unblinking and stubborn, she stared him down.

Again her courage surprised him. If he weren't careful, he was going to find himself liking her. Hatred was safer for Nicholas. And probably safer for himself.

Holding her eyes, Jake drew the receiver lightly against her, let it linger just on the curve of her breast, let her see the mockery in his eyes. "You're a good-looking woman. You must be used to guys making passes."

Disdain glinted in her eyes. "You weren't making a pass. You were bullying me."

"Is that what I was doing?" Clever woman. He *had* been bullying her. Not his usual style, but what the hell. Everything she did riled him. If he'd just met her under different circumstances he'd have liked her, wanted her, had her. His ethics, flexible though they were, wouldn't bend now on this point. He wouldn't yield to this treacherous desire that moved like lava through his blood, slow and sluggish and burning.

He was tempted, though.

"Make your call and get out of here." Ice clinked in the drawling flow of her voice. "Now."

"Got a telephone book? Yellow pages?"

"In the drawer by the counter." She gave him a wide berth.

He wondered what she'd say if he told her he could have her wrapped against him faster than she could blink. She would be small and supple, a miracle of softness and tenderness. No. Not tenderness. He couldn't expect tenderness from her.

"Here." She dropped the book before him. "And make it fast. I want you out of here before noon."

"Noon? You're not talking southern time, then. I'll be gone as fast as I can get the truck going."

"I'll call Willy's wrecker. He can tow you out of here." Blue fire blazed in her eyes.

Jake flipped through the yellow pages, looking for a service station. He had no intention of leaving, but he might as well fix his truck. Regardless of the satisfied look on her face, and the confident tilt of her slim neck, Sarah Jane Simpson wasn't through with him yet.

She wouldn't like knowing it, but she reminded him of a cheeky kitten he'd had long ago. Totally ignoring their differences in size and power, the hissing kitten would attack him, glowering in miniature fury. Later, satisfied by victory, she'd curl up at his feet, treating him like some outsized trophy she'd dragged in by sheer dint of effort.

Frowning, Jake remembered that easy comfort, the contentment of the familiar routine, a good time. His friend had let him stay for a while when Jake was fending for himself. He'd envied his buddy for a long time, but Jake had deliberately forfeited that kind of life, selling that undervalued serenity down the river. Nobody to blame for that except himself. It had been years since he'd thought about how he'd felt back then, always on the outside looking in with nothing of his own.

He ran his finger down the page. It was Nicholas, of course. Jake wasn't used to being responsible for other people. Drop in, move fast, get out faster. That was his style. What was he going to do about the kid? That question had tormented him for hours yesterday as he drove in the dark towards Sarah.

Jake stabbed his finger on a name. "Can you give me a lift to Moore Haven? There's a tire place there." He smiled grimly as her jittery urge to have him and Nicholas gone showed in her tapping fingers.

Sarah watched the smile and didn't trust it. He wanted something. Should she drive him and the boy into town? Well, she wasn't going anywhere with Jake Donnelly. What if she let Jake take her VW? He'd be a tough fit. Suppose he took off with it?

"You going to give me a lift?" His lean hip balanced against the counter.

She considered his tough face, its irritated scowl. She wouldn't trust him with herself but she was reasonably certain she could trust him with the car, and considering the state of the VW, maybe he'd be doing her a favor if he stole it. "No. You can use my car."

His smile spread brilliantly across his dark face. "Thanks." He shut the book, dropped it in the drawer. "Can I leave Nicholas here?"

Sarah didn't like that. She didn't want Nicholas with his little body around, his guileless enthusiasm rending her like a vulture's beak. What would she do with him? Jake's smile disappeared. What did he expect? Was she supposed to leap up and down and cry, "Oh wonderful! What fun!" for heaven's sake? Some women would. But she couldn't.

Still, the thought of Nicholas confined in the small car, carted around from one place to another disturbed her. He'd been carsick yesterday. He didn't need to be cooped up in a car again so soon.

Sarah watched Nicholas jump with gleeful abandon out of the old swing. She'd done the same thing when she was young. Sarah smiled at the memory of blazing sky and sun whirling over her head as she pumped higher and higher and then, eyes tightly closed, leaped into the void.

"Well?" Jake lounged against the door between the living room and the kitchen. "Hell, I'll even pay you to kid sit if it's such a big deal." He reached toward his pocket.

Sarah blanched. "Keep your money," she said in a chilly voice, forcing her words past the anger and humiliation as she remembered the way he'd flung the quarter at her. "I wouldn't take your money if I were starving!"

"Really?" One eyebrow arched. "Fastidious of you. I'd have thought otherwise."

Sarah's hand prickled, her blood roared in her head.

"No comment?" Jake shoved himself off the door.

She wouldn't cry. She wouldn't give him that satisfaction. She fought for control and dammed up her tears. He could stand there until hell froze over before he'd make her cry.

Like a net made up of the threads of her hurt and anger and his contempt, the moment stretched between them trapping Sarah. Jake reached to touch her. She slapped his hand away and pushed past him, jerking open the door. Breathing as hard as though she'd run a mile, she held the knob in her shaking hand. "Leave Nicholas. I'll watch him."

Jake nodded once, as though satisfied about something. Sarah kept the edge of the door and the edge of her anger between them as he walked out of the kitchen, his booted heels smacking on the wood of the living room.

Following him, she grabbed the car keys off the rack by the kitchen door and hurled them at him. He reached in back of him in midstride and caught the key ring as it jangled towards him. "I'll tell Nicholas he's staying, then." The screen door shut quietly behind him.

Sarah wrapped her arms around her middle and absorbed the shaking that slashed through her with Jake's departure. She didn't owe Jake anything. He was asking too much of her without even knowing it. Nicholas and his need sliced at her, but she'd function. Survival had been made up of worse moments than this. Emptying her mind, she sought control. *Don't think. Don't think.*

She'd give the boy what she could for the time being.

"Hey, sport!" Jake let the door close softly behind him as he yelled for Nicholas. Sarah puzzled him. Every time he thought he had a handle on her, she surprised him. He'd have bet the shine of tears over sea-blue eyes was real.

He knew he'd been vicious. Every time she retreated, he felt driven to slash at her. She hadn't cried, though.

The urge to comfort her startled him. He rubbed his chin hard, chasing away the imagined feel of her soft, wet skin against his palm. He wasn't interested in her pain, real or false. She'd get no sympathy from him.

"So, Jake, are we gonna get some worms and pop and go fishing?"

"Not right now, kid." Jake caught the flying body in his arms. "Hey. Careful, Nicholas. Warn a person before you jump on them."

"It's all right, Jake. I knew you'd catch me." Nicholas bumped Jake's chin companionably.

"Yeah, but warn me next time."

"Sure, Jake. Let's go fishing, now, okay?"

"Not right now, sport. We'll see about later."

"But, Jake—" Nicholas squirmed.

Jake explained the situation to him. For a long moment the boy clung to him, his small fist clutching Jake's collar. Powerless, Jake patted Nicholas's back. Jake wanted to leave, to take Nicholas with him and not come back. He wanted to let Sarah Jane Simpson keep her home filled with secrets and shadows. Jake swung Nicholas up on his shoulders and took long strides towards the orange VW under the porte cochere.

Absentmindedly Nicholas chewed on his fingernail.

"Stop that, sport." Looking at the painfully chewed nails, Jake winced.

"Oh yeah. I keep forgetting. It's just a bad habit I got. You got any bad habits?"

"Kid, you ask the craziest questions." Jake shook his head in frustration, thinking of several not-to-be mentioned habits. "I reckon I do. Maybe. I don't know!"

"Don't worry about it, Jake. You don't bite off your nails, anyway. I been watching."

"Good, now let's change the subject," Jake grunted.

"'Kay. I like it here, Jake. I've never been this near so much water. You gonna take me swimming while we're here? You said we'd stay while you took care of business." Nicholas thumped cheerfully on Jake's head.

How could he desert the boy now, with the whole mess still unsettled and himself the most unsettled of all? Jake's brain told him to run like hell, but deep inside a barely heard plea cried out when he looked into the woman's pain-filled eyes.

Jake perched Nicholas on the steps from the porte cochere to the front porch and looked at the face that had grown so important to him. He was trapped.

"You'll be back, right, Jake?" Nicholas hid the worry.

Just as his mother, Sarah, had hid her tears.

"I said I'd never go off and leave you, shortcake."

"But people disappear, Jake."

Sarah would never know if they disappeared. There'd be no one to tell her, no tortuous thread for her to unwind. He was a stranger she'd be glad to see the last of. And as for Nicholas... How could she not recognize her son? Wouldn't she recognize her own son if she were any kind of mother?

Nicholas wouldn't be abandoned the way Jake had been, not while Jake was alive. To hell with Sarah Jane Simpson. Jake smoothed Nicholas's hair behind his ear.

In his turn, Nicholas pulled on Jake's ear. "When you going, Jake?"

"Right now, sport. I'm going to fix our tire."

Nicholas wrinkled up his face. "You're crazy, Jake! First you cut the tire and now you're going to fix it?" He laughed, a clear, careless sound that echoed in the morning.

Jake opened the car door. "Yeah, sport, you're right on target. I'm crazy, that's for sure." Jake scrunched inside the car and said through the rolled-down window, "You mind Sarah, you hear?"

"Don't be a dope, Jake! But hurry back, okay?" The boy's expression wavered between excitement and anxiety as he stuck one finger in his mouth. "Hurry back!"

As Jake drove down the shell-lined driveway he watched the small figure in the rearview mirror waving goodbye. Jake swore and second-geared the VW out onto the highway.

Going to the kitchen window, Sarah heard Nicholas humming. He was shoveling sand with his hands, digging a hole. What was he up to? He wiped his arm across his face and returned to his industrious shoveling. Sarah's fingers strayed to the cutlery drawer. When she felt the cool metal in her fingers, she looked with astonishment at the big soupspoon. Why not?

She stroked the curved back of the old spoon, felt the dents. She'd put one there banging on a rock. Her cousin Buck had made another when he'd tried to use her forehead as a drum. There had been no meanness in Buck, who was a lawyer now, just too much energy. Smiling, Sarah pressed the metal slope to her face as she went outside to the child.

"Nicholas?" Her shadow fell over him.

"Mmm?" He squinted up at her.

Maybe Jake hadn't been negligent. She'd sent the boy out clean and he looked now as though he'd been in a pig wallow. Dirty and happy. "Could you use a spoon? To dig with?"

Sarah could see the wheels turning behind his bright eyes as he considered the offer.

"Yeah, maybe." He squatted on his heels. "Sure. I'm done digging right now, but it would make a great bridge, see?" He laid the spoon across the top of his hole and tamped dirt on each end. It was, indeed, a bridge, a shining, silver bridge.

Sarah dropped to her knees beside him, drawn despite her caution. "Where does the bridge go?"

His look was patronizing. "Bridges don't *go* anywhere, Sarah, ma'am. They just *are*, you know?"

Yes, she remembered. Everything didn't have to have a purpose. Some things could just *be*. "What did you do with the frog?"

He pushed on the spoon, testing its stability. He wouldn't look at her.

Sarah waited.

The lake was calm today. She'd have customers tonight. Fish would be biting out around the Birdcage even after last night's blowup. She should be exhausted, but lack of sleep hadn't hit her yet.

Nicholas wasn't going to answer her. She could identify with that kind of stubbornness. "Nicholas?"

He scratched his nose. "I turned him loose."

"Oh?" Sarah wondered why he was making such a mystery of the frog. She handed Nicholas two twigs.

He stuck one at the edge of the hole and broke the other into bits he scattered on the bottom. "He was homesick."

"I see." Sarah trailed sand through her fingers, sprinkled it on the broken twigs.

"He missed his daddy." Nicholas picked a periwinkle blossom and arranged it neatly down in the hole, away from the twigs and sand.

"Not his mommy?" Pain seared her memory.

"Nah."

Sarah touched the sand. A hard shell pricked her finger when she grasped it. "Where's his mommy?"

Nicholas didn't answer. His fingers were busy scrabbling in a patch of sandspurs. He chose several and ringed the top of the hole making a thick fence of the prickly burrs. "There. They'll be safe now."

"Will they?"

"Course."

Sarah knew the anonymous "they" wouldn't be safe, but she envied Nicholas's certainty. "Who's after them?"

He avoided her eyes. "Oh, nobody." He leaped to his feet. "Want to swing?"

He darted before, this way and that, mapping out his route. Sarah gave in. The warm air chased away fatigue.

Well, Nicholas was a treasure and she let him beguile her into forgetting that he'd be gone soon, pretending for a time that the past had never happened.

She knew she was foolish. She'd been foolish when she'd opened the door to Nicholas and the disreputable-looking Jake, but maybe God wouldn't begrudge her this moment that warmed her frozen heart with might-have-beens.

Sarah swung Nicholas until her arms were ready to drop. They walked down to the lake when an airboat roared in and captivated him. She couldn't ignore his wiggling eagerness, either, and begged a ride from the Seminole guide. Nicholas sat in the boat, his smile ear-to-ear.

When they returned, they ate tuna fish sandwiches out on the porch. Nicholas picked out the pickles and wadded them in his napkin. Downing the last of his iced tea—she wished she had milk—he flopped on the floor and focused on the revolving blades of the ceiling fan. Sarah had switched on the fan as the afternoon had become warmer. She leaned her head back on the chair, her feet near Nicholas. It was turning out to be a warm winter and the afternoons were downright hot. Not the best weather for fishing, but she'd make out. She wasn't solely dependent on income from guiding and boat rentals.

Nicholas interrupted her reverie. He was wiggling his legs in the air. "You like me, don't you, Sarah?" He rolled over on his belly and propped his chin on his hands as he waited for her answer.

Sarah couldn't give him a straight answer. "How could I not, Nicholas?" She evaded his gaze. Oh, she liked him. She did. And she'd like to roast the mother who'd let Jake take Nicholas off on this harebrained trip. Yet Sarah envied her.

He nodded. "Last night I thought you didn't like me, but it was just the dirt, huh?" At her startled look, he shrugged magnanimously. "I'm glad you like me. Jake's okay about stuff like dirt, but my dad didn't like me messing around much." His voice was obstinate. "He loved me a lot, so I didn't care."

"Of course he loved you, Nicholas." The pain was unbearable.

"My mom didn't." He rolled on the floor.

"Excuse me?" Sarah's thoughts scattered like sand in the wind.

"My mom didn't love me." He rolled from side to side, not concerned with the impact his words were having on her.

"Of course she does, Nicholas. Moms love their boys." Sarah's nails snagged on the wicker chair.

"Mine didn't love me," he insisted. He walked over to her chair, his knees bumping against her, those sharp-pointed little knobby knees.

"Oh, Nicholas, she must." As Sarah lifted him onto her lap, his bony body knocking and jabbing against her, she laid her chin on his head. Rocking him, rocking him, easing her own hurt and silencing her questions.

Nicholas looked up at her. "Are you crying, Sarah?" He rubbed his thumb under her eye.

"No."

"Looks like it." Inquisitive, he sat up straighter.

"No, must be my allergies." She let him go as he pulled off her lap, leaving her lap and arms empty. Sarah rubbed the wicker chair arm hard.

"That's too bad. I'm glad I don't have 'lergies." He opened the screen door and leaned out. "When's Jake coming back, Sarah?"

She wished she knew. She couldn't endure much more. Her mind was weaving fantasies.

When Jake rattled up the driveway, his headlights picked out Sarah down by the dock. She was hunched over her knees, looking out at the lake. A full moon shimmered in the dark of the night. Good. She'd put Nicholas to bed. She wouldn't kick them out tonight. He'd bought some time.

All afternoon Jake had driven around, delaying his return. After he paid for the new tire, he picked up smoked mullet and milk. Then, as an afterthought, figuring he might be in for a long night out in the truck, he added a six-pack of beer.

Now, after he shut off the ignition, he could hear crickets. "Sarah?"

She walked over to him. Leaning in the open window, she said, "You took your time, Donnelly." She twisted the door handle. "Come on out. I won't shoot." Her face was a pale circle in the moonlight. Weary lines etched the outside of her soft eyes.

Jake's skin prickled with alarm. What had happened? Sarah's edginess had vanished. She seemed all curves and softness in the wan light, an illusion. Losing himself in the watery light and her low voice, he had no defenses against this Sarah. He couldn't stay here.

"Come on in the house. Nicholas is upstairs asleep. But you knew that, didn't you?"

Her voice wrapped around his senses. "You timed your return very well. He's been asleep for half an hour. You're staying, of course." She paused, pointed to the sack of groceries in the VW. "I see you'd already made plans. Provisions?"

He nodded warily and removed the key. He'd been in control since he arrived, and while he'd been so cleverly tying her up with knots of responsibility, she'd undergone a change. Touched with shadows and mystery, her skin glowed in the moonlight. In spite of himself he wanted to touch it, see if it were satiny.

Jake walked beside her, shifting the paper sack to his outside arm. Once her arm brushed the hairs on his. She opened the screen door and beckoned him in. He followed.

In the kitchen she peered in the sack, got a bottle opener, plates and forks. "Want to eat on the porch? It's warm enough."

"Your house," Jake said, letting her take the lead. He'd follow her dance steps while she was in this mood. A bulldozer couldn't have pushed him out of her house at this moment, and he turned the heat of his anger to simmer.

He pulled the wicker table and chairs together and spread the fish on newspapers. "Beer?"

"Sure. Thanks." She sat yoga-style while she picked at the mullet with her fork. Then she smiled contentedly and pulled the succulent flesh off with her fingers, licking them free of clinging bits. "I love mullet, especially smoked."

The spicy scent rose between them, earthy, evocative, making Jake ache for long afternoons of lovemaking with rain drumming down. He shook his head, clearing his thoughts and gestured to the fourth fillet.

"I couldn't possibly... well, *possibly*," she amended, digging off one final white strip.

He wrapped up the bones and skin while she went to the kitchen.

She returned, carrying a knife and lemons. "Come on. Out on the stoop." She sliced the lemons and handed him one. Squeezing the juice over their hands, she rubbed hers together, sniffing them. "Nice."

Slick and wet her fingers twined. Jake wanted to slide his fingers between hers, touch the delicate webbing of lemon-bathed skin.

A long silence filled with possibilities thrummed between them, and then Sarah spoke. "Why did you lie about Nicholas's mother?"

Watching Sarah's face, Jake figured Nicholas had let something slip. She'd been setting him up. He should have known all the moonlight and magic were false. "I said three accusations of lying were enough. I didn't lie about Nicholas's mother." He hadn't, not really. He'd been very careful.

"Nicholas said his mother didn't like him."

Jake was as angry with himself as with Sarah. "She doesn't." He shifted into the shadows where he could watch her and not be seen.

"But he made it sound as if she were dead. You said his mother gave you permission to take Nicholas with you." Sarah's hands were folded tightly in her lap. "What's your game, Jake Donnelly? Why are you in my home?"

"Okay. I confess. I'm a drug dealer and the kid is my cover. All right? Call the cops." His voice was all calculated irritation.

She frowned and leaned back.

"Look, I said I had permission. I didn't say *who* gave me permission. Hell, I'd have brought references if I'd known I was going to wind up being given the third degree." Jake watched her face wrinkle as she tried to remember what he'd said.

Her eyebrows rose in disbelief.

His indifferent shrug was more convincing than an argument. "I'm sorry to destroy your swell, little conspiracy notions, but Nicholas's mother is alive. She just can't handle him right now after her husband's death."

"I don't understand." She twisted on the stoop towards him. A faint aroma of lemon rose to his nostrils.

Jake leaned back against the top stoop. "You're making something out of nothing." He sighed, wondering how much he could say.

He'd decided this afternoon that he wasn't going to tell her Nicholas was her son. Not now, maybe not ever. She was going to have to prove she could be trusted with the boy. If Jake had any doubts, *any*, he and Nicholas were hightailing it out faster than lightning could strike. If even one of the things he'd been told were true, she didn't deserve Nicholas, anyway.

Fairness and justice didn't matter. This time he held the cards. If he were some noble fool maybe he'd have a problem with his decision, but he couldn't afford any mistakes. Nicholas needed someone and Jake was all he had. He could be tough enough, cruel enough to disappear with Nicholas.

This time Jake could be God. What did he care about Sarah and her illusions?

He shifted and began again. "You and I have gotten off on the wrong foot. Everything I've said or done has been twisted by your fear, your suspicion." He cleared his throat. "I should never have stormed up to your door the way I did."

"No." She nodded.

He looked away. "I lack finesse sometimes."

"Oh, yes, I think we're in agreement there." Underlying her cool voice was laughter.

Jake went with it. Despite her doubts, she seemed willing to humor him. He was sure she had her own tainted motives. "And I'm mule-headed. Once I get the bit between my teeth, I'm hard to stop."

"Hmm."

"I'm not a nice guy."

Her hair lifted in the breeze and something changed in the night. "You're nice to Nicholas." Rivers ran deep in her voice, sweeping him along in their currents.

"Nicholas." Jake stretched his legs in front of him, waggled his feet.

"Yes, Nicholas." She stood in front of him, a small, indomitable figure smelling of lemon and flowers.

He almost admired her courage. Except that it, too, was an illusion.

"I don't like to talk about Nicholas," Jake continued, brushing away her thin cotton skirt that clung to his leg.

"You've made that very clear. *I* want to, though." Thinking of him and Nicholas and the story he'd told stirred a crazy thought up from the depths of Sarah's mind, one that explained everything except the impossible. But the idea sank below the surface when Jake stood up, powerful, his heat reaching out to her in the moonlight. She continued, "His situation baffles me. And there's something about him—"

As she moved in front of him, the cotton fabric of her skirt fluttered in the slight breeze, molding to her delicate curves. He wished he were someone else, anyone else, so he could wander off with her down toward the lake and find a shadowed, private spot where only the touch of skin on skin mattered. A place where he could stroke her skin, make her look at him with dazed blue eyes. As he watched her in the night, he sensed that with her he'd find something lost long ago.

He swore. What a fool he was making of himself. She was just a woman, and not even a nice one at that.

"Will you accept that what I'm going to tell you is as much of the truth as I can give you? That I mean no harm to Nicholas?"

"I know you wouldn't hurt him. He worships you." Sadness crept into her voice. "I might accept your version of the truth. It all depends." She looked up at the moon, her throat a silver silhouette in the dark.

"Good enough." Jake rose and stretched out the muscles of his back. "I *am* responsible for him right now, until his situation with his mother is resolved." He kept emotion out of his voice, knowing he didn't dare think of this woman in connection with Nicholas. "I *was* his father's friend, so I was asked to help. That's all I'm doing. Anything else you might be thinking, and God only knows what it might be, is just the result of my rudeness and your own imagination. I don't know what Nicholas meant by whatever he said, but I've told you the truth."

Jake touched the smooth strand of hair blown across her face. "And for my clumsiness, I apologize." Her eyelashes tickled the back of his finger as her eyes closed, opened. This time her beautiful eyes, Nicholas's eyes, looked at him with no wariness, no shutters. He couldn't afford to believe in her, for Nicholas's sake he couldn't, but his restless fingers moved with their own demands.

The bumpy fabric of her blouse slipped under his finger as it moved over the slope of her shoulder. He slid the fabric in small circles over her skin. Her shoulders were fragile wings under his hands. "No, don't," she murmured. He felt as though he were spreading lemon oil all over her, stroking it into her skin, her bones. He ran his thumbs down the indentation of her spine, pressing against her arching muscles. A muted whisper. His. An imperceptible sigh. Hers. For Jake the world tipped on its axis as he touched the hollows under her arms, urged her hands behind his neck. His breath came hard from his lungs, rasped. He needed her against him.

Sarah found herself pressed against the old tree, found herself touching the hard muscles of Jake's neck, lost herself in the feel of him against her. There was still something wrong about his story, but everything she'd denied herself for years was rolling in, drowning her with feelings. Questions could wait. She felt as vulnerable as baby turtles scuttling foolishly to the sea while the gulls circled hungrily overhead. Like the turtles, she raced for the breakers, defying death in a mad dash for life. That was what Jake was making her feel—that pulse-pounding, life-validating race for the sea.

He was a living pulse beat against her, and she clung to the life that throbbed in him and sent her own pulse surging against him. When he pulled her down on the swing with him, her skirt caught the breeze and lifted. She reached down to push it under them, but his hand stopped her, traced the edge of the skirt and smoothed under the light fabric. His palms met in back, cupping her, pulling her against him.

Through the nylon of her panties she felt the rasp of his hands, sensed the snag of callus against silky fabric. The tips of his fingers traced under the elastic edges, and she ached for his touch. She'd seen him touch Nicholas with tenderness and affection, and now his hands moved on her with a fierce tenderness that she needed. His hands slid over her thighs, thumbs meeting where she hurt for his touch. And he stopped.

Then the swing moved slowly forward, and she was lifted in the air, soaring against him. They wobbled for a moment, and Jake chuckled against her. He dug into the ground with his heels, and the swing twisted crazily. Sarah clung to him and he pulled her heels in back of him, locking her to him, locking her to his life pulsing on her, showing her how much he wanted her. One large, warm palm slid under the waistband of her panties and held her tightly while his free hand grasped the rope of the swing. His legs pushed hard on the ground, and Sarah felt the muscles of his thighs pumping under her as he sent them flying higher and higher in a mad spiral under the moon.

Sarah clung to Jake while the breeze blew back the sleeves of her blouse, billowed under her skirt, brushed her skin. The pounding of her heart and the giddy rush of sky over her were childhood relived with a difference. Jake pumped hard one more time, throwing his legs straight out and grabbing onto the rope with both hands while he fell backward, his head just missing the ground. Sarah collapsed against him, and there, upside down in slowing spirals and a tangle of arms and legs, he kissed her.

Sarah tasted anger and reluctant pity, but then Jake slanted his lips over her and hunger took her, leaving her breathless. His hunger, hers, she didn't know, didn't care while Jake's urgency sped her along.

But the pity in the kiss nudged her thoughts down a dark tunnel she'd run screaming from years ago.

Impossible. She didn't want to think. Wrapped in Jake's heat and urgency, she wanted to forget everything.

Something about Nicholas... Her thoughts seized her, compelled her.

Chapter Four

Sarah!"

The roaring in Sarah's head drowned out Jake's voice. His lips moved, but he was at the end of a long tunnel and was unimportant. Madness had come striking up at her like a shark from the deep, ripping her apart and sending her blood spurting into the dark waters. "Not again," she whispered, remembering the days and nights she'd spiraled in despair. Her son. Not dead. Not dead. She fought the fantasy.

She'd thought she was through with all that kind of thinking, but here it came again. It was too painful now to let that fantasy seize her and throw her down that tunnel she'd dragged herself from once. She couldn't do it again.

She'd been reckless to let Jake leave Nicholas with her.

"Sarah?" The roughness in Jake's voice pulled her back.

"I want to see Nicholas." Her cold hands pressed against her hot face. She tried to control the longing forcing her into irrational action.

"Why?" Jake chained her to him.

"Never mind!" Sarah shoved his arms away and tumbled off the swing. In the grip of her compulsion, she raced for the porch.

"Are you crazy?" Jake's grip sent her stumbling towards the shell-packed driveway. "You can't go running into Nicholas's room like this!"

His hands imprisoned her.

"What's the kid going to think?" Jake shook her.

That stopped her. Jake was right. She'd scare Nicholas. "I have to see him," she insisted, no longer sure why, just that she had to. She pushed at Jake, plucking futilely as his long fingers tightened around her wrists.

"Fine, you can. Just hold on a minute, okay?" Jake's voice held a gritty note she couldn't identify. Goose bumps raised on her arms.

"Don't treat me like an idiot!"

"Then don't act like one!" The yellow porch light lit up the shadowy planes of Jake's face and a reluctant compassion in it, a compassion that seemed as surprising to him as to her. He smoothed her hair behind her ears.

Anger plunged into melancholy. The past was dead.

"Sarah, what are you doing? You're not making any sense." Jake stroked her hair, and Sarah wanted to weep with frustration and dying anger.

"I want to see Nicholas." Her skirt whirled against her. Like leaves circling and whispering in the wind, her thoughts circled and returned, blurring the line between reality and possibility. "Oh, God, help me. I want my son!"

Jake's fingers clenched in her hair. She felt the small pain and welcomed it as a barrier against the greater pain of old loss.

"I don't know what you're talking about." On the rising wind, the clean scent of Jake's warm breath touched her face.

Sarah brushed away his hands. "Nothing makes any sense to me. I know you're lying to me. I don't know why. I know

you're here for some reason and I don't know what it is!''
Wanting to block out Jake's face, Sarah pressed her hands
against her eyes.

"Sarah, think. How could that be?" Jake's sigh whirled
away with the wind.

"I don't know," she answered bleakly.

Jake shook his head slowly. "Sarah, I didn't even know
you. You don't know me. There's no reason in the world for
me to show up on your doorstep."

"I'm not crazy. I'm not." Sarah wrapped her arms
around herself to still the shaking deep inside her. Maybe
she *was* crazy. What had made her think for a moment that
Nicholas could possibly be her son? Her son was dead, had
been dead for years. The State Department had sent her of-
ficial notification. They'd made sure she'd known. So sorry,
of course, but facts were facts.

"Nicholas and I are strangers to you. What else *could* we
be?" Jake's sandpapery voice scraped the night.

"I don't know. I can't think." She sighed. Her teeth
chattered.

"Listen, I've kissed a lot of women in my time, but I
usually get a different reaction. What did I do wrong?" Jake
shrugged when she only looked vacantly at him. "Sorry,
stupid joke." He opened the screen door. "Let's go inside.
Have some coffee? A beer?" He rubbed his head hard.

Sarah saw the calculation in his eyes and wondered. Jake
Donnelly was still playing games with her. She just hadn't
learned the rules. Ever since Jake and Nicholas had come
knocking on her door, her emotions had been yo-yoing to
the pull of Jake's hand on the string, and the child had
stirred up old grief. She'd drifted into make-believe with him
and carried it into reality.

"No. I'm going up to see Nicholas." Sarah snicked the
screened door behind them.

"No, you're not." Jake stepped between her and the front
door. "I won't let you." Darkness underlay his casual tone.

"There's no way on God's green earth you're going to stop me short of killing me," she said flatly. "And you're not a killer."

"I might be." His voice was as flat as hers had been.

Sarah looked him up and down, looked steadily in his uncompromising eyes while their colors shifted and changed. "Not in this life, you aren't." She pushed him aside. "I just want to see him, that's all." She was surprised by the ease with which she shifted his bulk. She would remember that later.

She gazed into the dark second story where the faint glow of a night-light softened the void. Nicholas had pretended he didn't want the pink shell plugged into the socket. "Sissy stuff," he'd scowled, but he hadn't turned it off. Sarah's heart pounded as her bare foot touched the carpeted staircase. Nausea churned her stomach. What was she doing? She had to control her behavior. She knew she was on the edge, knew it and couldn't stop. She had to see the child.

"By myself," she continued as Jake stayed close behind her.

"If you think for one minute I'm letting you go into the kid's room to wake him up and scare the living daylights out of him, you're really out of your cotton-picking mind!" Anger roughened Jake's voice. "I've been real patient, but this is the limit. He's my responsibility and I won't have you disturbing him!"

The protective passion behind Jake's anger startled her.

"I'm not going to disturb him. Surely you must know that?" Sarah halted in amazement. "How could you think I'd do such a thing?"

"How can I know what you'd do?" Jake countered, bitterness grooving lines around his mouth. "But I'm not letting you go up there by yourself."

"I don't understand you, at all," Sarah murmured. "You confuse me."

"That goes double, sweetheart, because you confuse the hell out of me." Jake shook his head. "Anyway, I know who Nicholas is and he's my business, not yours. No way am I turning you loose on him while you're in this state, so get that little notion out of your brain!"

It was the longest speech Sarah had heard from Jake. "Don't worry," she said. "I won't wake him up."

"Why do you want to see him, anyway? He's nothing to do with you! Nothing, that's what!" His furious whisper startled her as he pushed his face close to hers.

"I don't know," she wailed. "I don't know anything any more. I just want to see him! Can't you get that through your thick head?" Sarah took his head, trying to shake sense into him. Like black satin the strands of his hair moved through her fingers.

The air grew heavy between them. She could hear her breathing, his, the banging of the screen door. Jake moved a step closer, almost, she thought, against his will. Her fingers slipped out of his hair. "I'm sorry," she said. "I shouldn't have done that." She clasped her fingers together, still feeling the satin of Jake's hair between them.

"Oh, go on," he said tiredly. "But I'm going with you."

When he stepped up again, Sarah backed away from the implied threat and turned, reluctant now to ascend the stairs. Why did she feel this need to see Nicholas? She was out of control. No wonder Jake treated her like a threat. She was, but not to Nicholas, only to herself.

Her son had had no telltale birthmarks, no giveaway genetic markers. He'd just been a perfect little boy and she'd kissed his belly button with delight in his uniqueness as the doctor laid the small weight on her, the squinched-up face, the tiny fingers scrabbling against her and seizing her heart forever in their fragile grasp.

A whimper forced itself between her lips and she pushed Nicholas's door completely open, afraid now to see him because of the memories he would stir up, memories she'd tried to kill before they killed her.

Her heart was pounding, pounding. She looked down at the small, huddled form and, after all, what was there to see? Just a small, tired boy with his thumb in his mouth. A skinny little kid with a pointy face and ears that jutted out from his head. Her son? Of course not. In the clear light of rational thought, she knew better. Someone's son. But not hers.

Tears slipped silently down her face as she watched the sleeping child. She gripped her hands tightly together against the urge to take him to her. She'd been right to stay away from children, from entanglements of any kind. Oh, she'd been right to detach herself from all the pain people brought with them. She still wasn't strong enough.

"He's such a little boy," Sarah whispered. "My son would have been the same age." Blinded by her tears, she leaned forward, wanting to touch his thin cheek, wanting to tuck the blanket under his chin, wanting something she was never going to have.

Jake's callused fingers stopped her. "Don't," he ordered harshly.

"Oh, please, don't be cruel," Sarah whispered. Jake's fingers dropped from her arm as if she'd scorched him with a red hot iron. His dark form moved away into the shadows of the room and she bent to Nicholas.

His skin was cool to her fevered touch and he sighed as she brought the blanket securely around him. She'd had so few chances to comfort her own son in the night. He'd been so small, wrapped in his blanket as she'd carried him through— "Satisfied?" The burr of Jake's voice interrupted her thoughts.

Gratefully she turned to him, eager to escape the memories. "Satisfied?" She laughed, a tear-choked harshness to her own ears. No wonder Jake thought she was crazy. She rubbed the salty tracks of her tears. "If you only knew!"

"So tell me," Jake invited in a distant voice as he walked abruptly out of the room.

Sarah lingered, sorting out her thoughts. Nicholas and Jake were forcing her to face her memories, face herself and her own failures. Her failure to keep her son safe. But she'd done everything, *everything* in her power, and in the last analysis everything hadn't been enough.

Kneeling beside Nicholas's bed, she watched the movements of his closed eyes as he dreamed and breathed in the small-boy smell of him.

She remembered his cuddling up at her feet, his fear that she didn't like him. She remembered the whole of the day as he'd wormed his way past her walls, leaving her raw and aching. That was why she'd gone streaking to see him. Wishful thinking rising up from long-buried hopes and pain. For the first time since she'd lost her son she'd let herself be vulnerable, and memories and moonlight had made her crazy. Now the child curled near her hand was forcing her to face that pain and loss.

Another time she sensed Jake hovering outside the door. He hadn't really trusted her alone with Nicholas, after all. Silent moments drifted past. As she knelt there watching Nicholas, she mourned all the lost moments she'd never had with her own son. Nicholas's fist closed around her hand and she felt the ice in her heart crack.

Sometime later she rose from her cramped position and walked down to the kitchen. Jake lay stretched out on her sofa, but she didn't say anything to him. She poured herself a glass of iced tea, taking pleasure in the sight of the cool amber flowing against the clear ice, taking pleasure in the music of ice cubes clinking against one another.

"Do you want a beer now, Jake?" she called before she looked up at the clock and saw that once again it was after midnight. "Or not?"

"Yeah, I could use a beer." Jake appeared at the door but didn't come in. "If you don't mind."

"No problem. I wouldn't have offered if I did." Sarah smiled at him even as she wondered at his detachment. If he were as tired as she was, though, and as confused by her behavior as he had to be, he had every right to withdraw. "What I do want to offer you, though, is an apology."

"Forget it," he snapped. "I don't want an apology. Just a beer. Please," he added, not looking at her.

"Well, I want to explain why—"

"Listen, Sarah—" He spoke at the same time, then shrugged. "Never mind." He took the beer from her hand and walked back toward the living room.

Jake felt like slamming his fist through a wall. He'd never forget the sight of Sarah's soft face as she looked at Nicholas. He'd carry the sight of that moment with him to the grave. Her pain had clawed at his resolve, and he'd almost broken down and admitted that Nicholas was her son. But he'd hardened his heart and, leaving the room, saved himself. And saved Nicholas, too, he reminded himself.

He watched Sarah collapse into the faded rocking chair. He wanted to yell at her; she had no right to make him feel guilty after what she'd done. No, he wasn't going to feel guilty. Tough if she was all torn up. Life was tough. For everybody. He sat as far away from her as possible and leaned his head back against the sofa. She'd looked so defeated and vulnerable with her soft hair spread on the pillow next to Nicholas. Jake had to kill that something in himself that was drawn to her anguish and her softness or he was going to end up failing Nicholas.

He rubbed his forehead with the wet, cold bottle and shaded his eyes. "Well?" he began.

"Yes, well . . ." Her husky voice trailed off. If that voice could be bottled and sold as an aphrodisiac, someone would make a fortune. Jake shut his eyes, but he could still hear her and couldn't escape what her voice did to him.

"I kissed you, you kissed me back—not bad but nothing special," he lied. "Nothing to cause what happened next."

She'd sent him into an absolute cold sweat when she'd gone running to see Nicholas. Jake had been paralyzed by inaction for the first time in his life. He hadn't known what she was going to do. Lost in their kiss until the cold water of her words snapped him back to reality, back from the sense of homecoming in her softness, he'd forgotten who and what she was. "You want to say anything, go ahead. If not, let's forget it, and chalk it up to bad technique on my part."

"I owe you an explanation."

He surged to his feet and turned his back to her, looking out at the dark yard. He should never have come here. "I told you, you owe me *nothing*. You looked after Nicholas for me, gave him a bed for the night. I'd have taken one, too, if you'd offered." He faced her with a deliberately nasty grin.

"Stop it. Why are you being so crude?" she cried. "You turn it on and off like a switch, so just stop it. I want to talk about what happened."

"Drop it," he persisted.

"You need to know!" Her small hand touched his bare arm.

Jake yanked away from the touch that went right to his toes and curled his insides. "Yeah. I guess I do." He paced the length of the room. "So go on. You have a son, right?" He refused to look in her direction. He was crackling and sparkling with anger, guilt. And desire. That's all. Just a good, old-fashioned itch for a woman. Nothing more. He crossed his arms and leaned his head against the front door leading to the porch. He'd listen to her lies.

"I . . . have a son." Her voice was thready but controlled.

He rubbed his arms. "Yeah?"

The quiet house wrapped them in its timelessness, surrounded them with security and history and made him aware of his own emptiness. It was a house whose voice seduced him as much as Sarah's did.

"Had." Her long, drawn-out sigh settled in the corners of the room and in the bleak spaces of his hard heart.

"So tell me about it." Jake wondered how soon he could wake Nicholas up and leave.

"He would have been six next month." She pressed her fists to her chest. "Funny, isn't it?" He saw the gleam of tears in her eyes. She moved to the table by the chair, slid the bowl of roses back and forth.

"No, not funny. What happened?" Jake sat down again on the couch, tenting his fingers over his face, watching her troubled movements around the room as she adjusted pictures, stacked magazines and rubbed her fingers over shining wood surfaces.

"Somehow I always thought he was alive. Prayed. Hoped." She opened the door and looked out onto the porch where the low rumble of thunder over the lake and lightning low on the horizon disturbed the peace of the house. Swept in with the wind, the heavy, sweet smell of orange blossoms filled Jake's nostrils. He waited.

"You see," she turned toward him and the wind whipped her hair forward and tossed her skirt around her smoothly rounded hips and legs, "I never believed them. They told me he'd been killed, but I didn't believe them." She moved toward him, her hands outstretched. "I would have known if he were, wouldn't I? In here?" Her clenched hands rose fiercely to her heart. "Wouldn't I?"

Jake shrugged. "Maybe not. Maybe," he added reluctantly, unable to resist the appeal of those clenched, trembling hands.

"From the moment I opened my door to you and Nicholas, it's been as though I've been moving through a dream. I can't explain it, but just before you knocked I was dreaming, oh, I don't even remember what it was, but I felt so happy, and then you scared me when you pounded on the door and nothing has made sense from then on."

"I was rude, that's all."

"Yes, you were, but it was more than that. I think it was being thrown off balance. Suddenly I started seeing things differently. Did you ever look at someone's face upside down, so that the mouth is on the top? You view the person so strangely then. Your perception changes."

He knew what she meant. "So?"

"Some part of me has always refused to accept that my son was . . . anyway, when I spent so much time with Nicholas, time I'd never had, would never have, with my son, something snapped into focus and all of a sudden, I don't know, it was as if the only thing that explained your appearance and the whole dreamlike quality was that somehow, against all rational explanation, Nicholas was my son."

Jake tried to ignore the hoarseness running under her calm voice. "Yeah, I can see how that might happen."

"And then when you kissed me—you had a look in your eyes that you get when you look at Nicholas." She looked pleadingly at him. "It was ridiculous, I know, but can't you see how it made sense to me?"

"Not really," he muttered, trying not to let her voice slide under his skin.

"I was crazy for a few minutes." Sarah curled up in the chair and tucked her legs under her.

Her bare toes with their pink polish peeked shyly at him. If things were different, if she weren't Nicholas's faithless mother . . . "Forget it," he said.

"But I want to thank you," she added.

A bleak laugh escaped him. "I'm the last person you should thank."

"You see, I'd avoided pain for so long that I didn't feel anything any more. And that's not living. I'll never get over the loss of my son. I think about him every day."

Jake's conscience twisted the knife. Did she deserve what he was doing? What if everything Ted had said was true? The Sarah who sat curled in front of him surely wasn't the same Sarah Ted had told him about. Had she gone off the deep end? That would explain the story Ted had stuck to with his dying breath. Explain it, but would it make her a fit mother even now for Nicholas? If she'd left him once, she'd do it again. Leopards didn't change their spots.

"What about your husband?" he said.

"It's a long story."

"I'm a good listener." He wanted to hear how she'd explain what she'd done, but he knew she couldn't.

"But some things aren't worth talking about. He's dead. Killed with my son." Her mouth tightened.

"How did it happen?" Jake felt like a disembodied voice in the confessional. Like a priest, he wouldn't be satisfied until she spilled out the horror of what she must have done. Had done.

"Just one of life's tragedies, that's all." Her voice dwindled into silence.

"What do you mean?" He wouldn't let her off now.

"It doesn't matter," she cried. "They both died and they didn't have to! They would never have died like that if—"

Jake moved restlessly. He was so close. "If what, Sarah, if what? How did they die? Tell me."

The intensity in his voice must have drawn her back from wherever she had gone, for she glanced at him and then away as she said, "In a little country in the Middle East, one of those countries perpetually at full boil. They were there and they died. And I was here."

Her last three words sent chills over him, but then a sizzle of lightning raised the hair on the back of his neck and he smelled ozone.

"That was close," Sarah said. "Will Nicholas—"

Just as she spoke, Nicholas hove into view like a small ship racing for port and launched himself into Jake's arms. "Hey, Jake." His mouth stretched wide in a yawn. "Hey, Sarah."

"Hey, yourself, sport."

"And hay's for horses, I know, Jake." Nicholas's eyes were wide open even as he yawned from ear to ear. "What you and Sarah doing down here?" He grinned at Sarah who smiled back.

Her smile was filled with such warmth and welcome that Jake hungered. No one except Nicholas had ever smiled at him like that, welcomed him with such unreserved affection.

"Not much, Nicholas. Did the lightning wake you?" Her voice was low and comforting, the sound of hot cocoa and marshmallows and fuzzy slippers.

"Nah, I just missed Jake." He slid his arm around Jake's neck and Jake gave him a small squeeze. "I'm not afraid of lightning." Nicholas looked at Jake. "Jake might be."

"What would I do if I were, kid?"

"Maybe you could ask me to keep you company?" Nicholas peered earnestly at Jake through tangled eyelashes. "I wouldn't mind much if you wanted me to, Jake," he added generously.

Jake liked the feel of Nicholas in his arms, the sleepy trust. He'd been ridiculously touched and pleased when the kid had come vaulting into his arms, bypassing Sarah without a glance. Jake had always thought kids automatically went to females for comfort. Over the top of Nicholas's head, he looked at Sarah and surprised such a look of yearning that he was jarred. What in God's name was he doing?

"How about it, Jake?" Nicholas put both his hands around Jake's face just as Sarah had done and brought Jake's attention to him. "Then you wouldn't have bad dreams, either."

"Do you have bad dreams, Nicholas?" Sarah had come over to them, her hand gently touching Nicholas's foot, which hung over Jake's arm.

For a moment Nicholas didn't answer. Jake could tell Nicholas was thinking through the possibilities before he finally spoke. "I'm too big for bad dreams, Sarah."

"Gosh, Nicholas, I have really bad dreams sometimes, and I'm a lot older than you." Sarah tugged at Nicholas's big toe and Jake felt the small movement as if she'd touched him.

"You do? Well, I have bad stories in my head sometimes. But they're not bad dreams," he insisted.

Jake chuckled. The kid was hardheaded and filled with pride. "Look, sport, how about something to drink before you head back up to bed?"

Nicholas slid slowly to his feet. "I think you should come with me, Jake. You'd feel a lot better if you did." He tugged at Jake's hand.

Looking at Sarah, Jake silently asked permission. For Nicholas's sake, he'd play a civilized waiting game, waiting for her to make a mistake. She would. He knew it in his bones.

Nicholas turned to her. "You can come, too, Sarah, but Jake takes up a lot of room."

Sarah's ears turned bright pink. "Um, thanks, Nicholas, but, um, that's all right. Tell you what, I'll let you take Jake upstairs and then I'll bring you some milk."

"Come on, then, Jake." Nicholas pulled Jake to the stairs before adding, "I don't mind if you carry me up."

"Here you go. Hang on, goofus." Jake swooped Nicholas up into a fireman's hold and took the stairs two at a time. Nicholas smothered a giggle against Jake's shirt.

When Sarah walked in with warm milk, Nicholas was half-asleep, his hand gripping Jake's tightly.

"Here, I'll take that," Jake said, cupping his free hand around the yellow mug. He watched Sarah's face as she looked at Nicholas. She didn't fuss over him, but her face was filled with something that might pass for tenderness, he thought peevishly.

"If he doesn't drink it, just leave it on this coaster. I'll get it in the morning."

Jake put the milk down on the nightstand. "Okay. I'll wait until he's asleep and then—"

A crack of lightning interrupted him.

"No, Jake, you gotta stay here," Nicholas said and hung on to Jake's hand.

"Of course he does, Nicholas. Anybody could see Jake needs you on a stormy night like this." Sarah's bright eyes sparkled at Jake as she made a teasing face.

She was so much like Nicholas. But with a major difference, he thought, as he watched her skirt pull tight against her thigh as she sat next to Nicholas on the bed.

Jake went warm all over.

"G'night, Sarah," Nicholas yawned. "Let's go fishing tomorrow." Then, like a member of royalty, he conferred a supreme honor. "You can kiss me goodnight. I don't mind, but I *am* too big for kissing, you know."

Jake heard Sarah's whisper as she leaned over Nicholas. "I know, and too big for bad dreams. But you're only going to have good stories because Jake will be right here. He needs you." Sarah's lips touched Nicholas's cheek very gently.

"You better kiss Jake, too, or you'll hurt his feelings," Nicholas added as Sarah got up to leave.

She looked startled. "Oh, I think Jake's definitely too big for goodnight kissing." Her whole face flushed.

Raising his eyebrows, Jake shrugged. "Yeah, but you don't want to hurt my feelings." He knew he was playing with fire, but he wanted that illusory warmth momentarily.

Her kiss was a cool butterfly touch on his skin, and it made him lonelier than he'd ever been in his life as she shut the door behind her.

"Turn loose just a sec, sport, so I can get my boots off, and then slide over. I'll stay until you fall asleep."

Jake shucked off his boots and stretched out. Nicholas was already half-asleep. Jake shifted uncomfortably. Who'd believe the kid could spread himself all over a whole bed like that? Jake plumped up the pillow, the same one where Sarah's head had lain earlier, and a faint scent of her wafted to him. He slammed the pillow grimly under his head and refused to think of how she'd looked face to face with Nicholas.

How could he take Nicholas away from her?

Nicholas's foot worked its way back over to Jake's arm. Cold little toes slid up and down. He reached down carefully and took them in his hands, warming them. Odd how the kid liked him, had from the first. Jake hadn't thought the kid would have trusted him so completely right off, but he'd stuck by his side like superglue from the beginning.

How could he go away and leave Nicholas behind?

Jake didn't know how long he lay there holding Sarah's son by the toes and breathing in the faint, sweet smell of her on the pillow and waiting for her son to fall safely asleep before he went to his own bed, but he knew he felt completed in a way he never had before. An ache uncoiled in him with the knowledge that it could only be temporary.

Some time during the night, after he'd moved to the other bed, a soft knocking at the front door woke him. He stretched and stirred, alerted by Sarah's lighter voice answering deeper, male tones. Slipping out of bed, Jake padded to the window and watched as Sarah walked down to the dock with two men loaded down with fishing gear. The boat coughed once and disappeared into mist.

He frowned. What was she doing? How could he leave Nicholas with a woman who disappeared at all hours of the night? Satisfaction uncurled in his stomach.

Brooding in the silence and watching the boat disappear with Sarah, Jake fancied that the light winked mockingly at him as dark swallowed the orange glow.

Chapter Five

So long, guys. Glad you got some fish!'' Sarah said as she helped Charlie and Walt unload their gear. For years the Chicago dentists had been flying down in their Cessna to Okeechobee. ''Hope someone doesn't take you for a bear, Charlie, with your shaggy beard.''

''Not a chance. A bear's prettier!'' Charlie threw his rods in the station wagon.

''Too bad about the weather, but the fish weren't out,'' she said to Walt.

''No problem. Got enough to eat now and pack the rest in ice for the plane.'' Walt took the bait buckets from Sarah. ''You ever gonna get some fella to help out around here?'' He grunted as he hefted the tackle box out of the boat. ''A looker like you shouldn't have any trouble roping in a steer.''

Sarah laughed. ''I'm not into ranching, Walt, but if I could find a man as good-looking as you, I'd have him in a second.''

''And if my old woman wasn't such a tiger in bed, doll, and me so old, I'd buy you the ring today!''

"If Betty could hear you—"

"Just so long as I keep her happy." Walt patted his gray hair. "Snow on the mountain, fire inside!"

Sarah rolled her eyes.

"Believe me, she loves every minute of it!" Walt hugged Sarah. Sixtyish and burly, he reminded her of her dad, who had died while she was in college. "See you around, gorgeous. Charlie, let's go." Walt handed her a folded wad of money.

"Too much, you only fished one time." Sarah handed him back three twenties.

"Keep it, doll. It was worth it just to see your pretty face. Anyway, we wouldn't ever get fish if it weren't for you." Walt shoved the money back in her fist. "What's a rich, old fool like me going to do with all my money? I'd rather give it to a pretty woman any time!" Walt squeezed behind the steering wheel, and the two men waved as they pulled out of the driveway.

Walking back to the house, Sarah breathed early morning dampness deep into her lungs. Whistling quietly and thinking about her uninvited guests, she dropped her muddy shoes at the door and headed for the shower.

Jake still puzzled her. She wasn't stupid. She knew he had a reason for landing on her doorstep. She hadn't figured out what it was yet, but she would. If he thought she believed his story, he had another think coming.

Until she knew why he'd knocked on her door, she'd let Jake stay, but she wasn't going to drop her guard again the way she had last night. She'd been vulnerable to his kisses, and the day spent with Nicholas had triggered those impossible thoughts. In the clear light of morning, her reactions seemed even stranger.

Sarah shook her head as she walked quietly up the stairs. She'd figure it out. The morning sunlight cast its benediction on the old hall carpet. She couldn't resist poking her head in where Nicholas and Jake slept. With the tip of her finger, she edged the door open.

The long, heavily muscled length of Jake's body met her eyes and startled her into immobility. His briefs gleamed whitely against his brown skin. Touched by faint light, his muscles coiled under that skin, tempting her fingers to touch and see if they were as sleek and powerful as they looked. Jake's uplifted arm draped over his face, pulling his powerful chest into profile and making concave the ridges of his stomach where dark hair narrowed towards that bright whiteness which drew her eyes.

Jake's empty hand, a muscular bridge, stretched towards Nicholas's rumpled and equally empty bed, but through the open window Sarah heard the boy's humming.

Sarah wouldn't have moved for any amount of money. The sight of Jake's powerful maleness, defenseless now in sleep and tenderness, pulled at her. Just as she inhaled, Jake's arm moved, and she saw his watchful brown eyes open.

She didn't know what to expect, whether he would cover himself or perhaps be angry. What she didn't expect was his lazy smile.

"My, what big eyes you have, Grandma," he whispered.

Before she realized what she was doing, she whispered back, "The better to see you with."

Jake's mouth curved, and Sarah went hot as she realized what she was saying.

"Naughty Red Riding Hood," he murmured, still not moving as silence settled around them.

"It was the wolf's fault," she retorted. "He tempted her."

"Do I, Sarah," Jake whispered, "tempt you?" His chest moved as he breathed deeply.

Melancholy shaded his banter and made her rethink her smart-alecky retort. "Maybe," she replied, caught in the spell cast by quiet and sleepiness.

"Only maybe?"

His bleak smile touched her and made her forget all her resolutions.

"Think how it might be between us, Sarah."

She did. She thought about how it would be to stroke those long ropes of muscled male, how it would feel for him to touch her with those big hands, how it would be to lie draped over him, how it would be to say goodbye to Jake...and to Nicholas.

Before she could shake her head, Nicholas's rat-a-tat-tatting on the tin wash bucket shattered the hush, and Jake added, "Well, can't blame a man for trying, sweetheart, but don't surprise a man when he's waking up and vulnerable to a sexy woman and not expect him to let you know how he's feeling. Sorry if I shocked you." Irritated, he lifted up on his elbows. "You better go, Sarah, before I really try to tempt you." He placed one thickly muscled thigh over the side of the bed.

"You don't shock me." Sarah tilted her head.

"No?" He stood up.

Sarah didn't move. His briefs rode low on the bones of his hips and she felt overwhelmed by the sheer force of his maleness. He was big, tough, and he wanted her. The contemplation of how it would be to be wanted—and taken—by him kept her standing there as he moved toward her. Even before he touched her, she felt his heat.

He gripped her shoulders for a second. "I'd like to kiss you silly, Sarah Jane Simpson." He pushed her gently against the door. "You know that, don't you?" Dark and heavy, his words blanketed her.

She nodded.

"I'd kiss those pink lips until they were red and swollen and I'd tempt you, Miss Simpson, oh, yes, I'd tempt you down paths I don't think you've ever gone." His head lowered to hers.

Clean and sharp, his scent enveloped her. Being seriously tempted by Jake began to sound like something she wanted very much.

"And you know what, sweet Sarah? I think you'd lead me down paths I've never gone, either." His voice was low and sad. "But I don't know if I could find the way back."

She didn't have the slightest idea what he meant, but he sounded so desolate that she touched her fingers to his face. His bristly cheek rubbed the palm of her hand, sending tingles through her.

"Would you leave me there, Sarah, or would you take my hand and show me the way home?" He rubbed and rubbed, but so lightly that the touch was a caress against the sensitive skin of her wrist. "And if you left me there, Sarah, what would be left for me?" For a moment he buried his face in her hand.

"Jake, I don't know what you mean," Sarah whispered. Jake was still for a moment and then he answered, but so quietly that she wasn't sure she'd heard him. "I want you, Sarah Jane Simpson, that's what I mean, and I'd like to take you right now in your sweet-smelling room and fill up my senses with you. And then I'd want to have you all over again, and that, sweetheart, scares the daylights out of me." He laughed and she felt his breath in her palm.

"It's not possible. You're just passing through, you and Nicholas."

"Ah, yes. Nicholas." Jake straightened.

"You have to take Nicholas back home."

"But what if it weren't like that, Sarah? What then?" His fists pressed on either side of her face against the door. "If we're talking about fairy tales, wouldn't that be a swell one? Happy ever after and all that?"

Sarah felt the brush of his crisp leg hair against her thigh.

"Weren't you the kind of little girl who curled up under that oak tree out there with your illustrated *Brothers Grimm*?" His fingers slid to her hair. "I can see you out there, you know, dreaming your dreams, your legs dangling over the edge of your swing. Did you dream of a knight on a white horse coming to sweep you off your feet?''

He slipped the strands of her hair between his fingers and she turned her head away. A Jake bent on serious tempting was a very dangerous Jake. All her bones had turned to jelly.

"I'm not a knight on a white horse, Sarah, but I could sweep you off your feet." Low and rough, the words invaded her senses. "I could make you forget about fairy tales for a while." His thumbs touched the skin of her eyelids. "Wouldn't you like that, Sarah, being swept off your feet?"

His face was so near that she couldn't think. Oh, yes, she could see how she'd like having Jake sweep her off her feet, leaving her no time to think of consequences, no time to think of the future. He could do it, too.

He smiled and touched her nose with his. "Eskimos kiss like this. Nice, isn't it?"

"Hmm." She'd never known her nose had so many nerve endings and all of them connected to some aching place inside of her. "Very." She rubbed her nose against his.

"See how easy it would be, sweetheart? See how nice?"

"But *nice* isn't quite the word, Jake." She turned her head.

"No? And here I'm trying so hard to be a nice guy." His lips moved near her ear, and the tip of his tongue touched the rim. Briefly. Too briefly.

"Ah, *that's* nice, Jake." She shivered.

"I thought it might be." He chuckled as his elbows bent and he lowered his chest to her, his hand sliding to the back of her head and tugging at the braid of her hair, urging her head back.

Her heart was racing and her mouth was dry. She'd never wanted a kiss in her life the way she wanted Jake's kiss. His lips hovered over hers, waiting.

It was the waiting that did it. Her pulse thundered so hard that she couldn't hear anything except her own heart. She leaned forward, met his lips with hers, surrendered to the wild surge. And then she opened her eyes. Sharp with desire and judgmental, Jake's intent eyes pierced her to the depths of her being, so much hunger and emptiness and caution looking back at her.

He couldn't know how naked he was. Sarah drew back. She wasn't ready for Jake and his hunger. The stakes were too high.

"No, Sarah?" His lips moved lightly against hers. "Perhaps you're right." He lifted himself away. "But it would have been nice, I promise you." His smile was rueful, frustrated.

"I know." Already Sarah regretted her decision, but the moment had passed. She'd finally gotten smart. She was in no shape to take on Jake Donnelly.

Jake drew his finger lingeringly down her throat. "Get out of here, Sarah, while I can still remember why I should let you."

"But—"

"*Now*. Because if you stay, I won't let you go a second time. I won't remember that it's not *nice* to seduce little girls who dream of knights on white horses, sweet Sarah, so go while you can." He opened the door and shoved her out.

Sarah looked at the closed door for a second, her whole body aching, feeling the lure of Jake's longing and need. Her lips trembled on her whisper, "You're a fraud, Jake Donnelly." Her fingers burned where they brushed the door. As she turned to her room, she heard Jake call out the window to Nicholas.

Gathering up underwear, sleepshirt and socks, Sarah stretched. She couldn't remember being this drained in years.

She couldn't get Nicholas out of her mind, and Jake— sure, Jake was shaking her world like a dog with a rag doll. It would be nice having the two of them around for a while, she thought drowsily.

Barely awake, she leaned her forehead against the shower wall, smiling as she soaped and rinsed. Jake was like a half-wild dog, circling around a camp fire but reluctant to approach its warmth, but with Nicholas, Jake came in out of the cold.

Throwing the sleepshirt over her still damp body, she tumbled into bed. If she could just sleep for four hours now, she'd be a new woman. Oddly, her last coherent thought as her head hit the pillow and stayed there was about Nicholas's ears.

Through layers of sleep-chained consciousness, Sarah heard voices. She wanted to put her feet on the floor, knew she was going to stand up any second.

"Let her sleep, sport. She's tired." A door closed quietly.

"She wouldn't want to sleep, Jake. Sarah likes to get up and do things. She told me so. She's gonna be real mad if we leave her out."

"I don't think she'll mind if we make breakfast while she sleeps. Let's go down and see what we can find."

"This is a big mistake. Sarah promised we'd go fishing today, and she really wants to. I told her I'd bait her hook." Nicholas's voice faded away, and with an insistent tug sleep summoned Sarah.

Downstairs, Jake opened cupboard doors. The neatly lined shelves didn't surprise him. Flour, sugar, oatmeal, all in tidy glass jars. Safe...unlike Sarah. He'd let her get to him again, and he couldn't afford to. He had to keep his hands off her. He'd seen the wad of money in her pocket. God only knew where she'd gotten that kind of cash. "What's in the fridge, sport?"

"Lots of good stuff. Some weird stuff. How about a sandwich? I used to make sandwiches for me and Dad." Nicholas tilted his head inquiringly.

It was just the way Sarah tilted her head. "I think we need rib-sticking food if we're going fishing. Any eggs in there?"

"I don't like eggs, Jake. You ever think about eggs? I saw a movie once. You know where eggs come from, Jake? Yuck." Nicholas screwed his face up in disgust.

"You got a point there." Jake tried not to laugh. "No eggs, then."

"How about a jelly sandwich? Here's that guava stuff Sarah makes. It's sticky. I had some yesterday."

"You're really big on sandwiches, aren't you?" Jake squatted down to look in the refrigerator.

"Sure. They're great. Look, Sarah's even got squishy white bread. I love squishy bread." Nicholas squished the bread.

Jake took the bread. "What about cereal?"

"Nah. A sandwich."

"A sandwich, huh. Let me think a minute." Jake poked behind some boxes, opened the meat drawer. The kid was too skinny. He needed a good breakfast. "Okay, but it has to be a Jake's Special. Fair enough?"

"Sure. What you want me to do?" Nicholas pulled a chair over to the counter. "You know something, Jake? Me and you do neat stuff together," he confided, leaning against Jake.

"Yeah?" Jake shifted to make Nicholas comfortable and then lopped off margarine and tossed it into a cast-iron skillet. The lump sizzled and melted.

"Dad didn't do stuff. But he was tired a lot," Nicholas added loyally.

"That was tough." Jake slapped three pieces of bread in the skillet and topped them with ham and cheese before slicing a brilliant red tomato onto the cheese and finishing each sandwich with a slice of bread.

"Jake, I'm hungry. When are these Specials gonna be ready?"

"We have to flip them over and fry the top side." Jake handed a spatula to Nicholas. "Think you can do that?"

Nicholas gripped the spatula in a tight fist and jammed it under one of the sandwiches. Tomato and bread flew sideways.

"Slow down, sport." Jake held Nicholas's hand under his bigger one and showed him how to ease the spatula all the way under while flipping quickly. Nicholas's eyebrows met in concentration.

Jake felt a pang as he thought about leaving Nicholas. He could teach the kid a lot. Nicholas picked up things like a sponge. He couldn't leave him with a mother who disappeared during the night. "Good job. That's the way," he encouraged, as Nicholas flipped the other two sandwiches.

"I know," Nicholas asserted. "It's not hard. I'm gonna get the sodas now, Jake. You can make coffee if you want it, but soda's better."

"Whoa!" Jake grabbed the tail of Nicholas's shirt. "No soda for breakfast, kid. Milk. Or juice."

Nicholas frowned. "Why not?"

"Not good for you."

Nicholas jammed his fists on his nonexistent hips and glared at Jake. "You say that a lot, Jake, but you eat doughnuts and stuff. *And* you drink soda."

"But not for breakfast. Here," Jake handed him a glass. "Milk."

Nicholas took it and trudged to the refrigerator. "Dumb stuff, milk. You ever think about milk, Jake? You know where it comes from?"

Coming in on the tail end of the exchange, Sarah stifled her laugh.

"Jake's right, Nicholas," she said as she stepped inside. "You need milk. When you get older, you can drink what you want."

"How old I gotta be?"

"Oh, about as old as Jake, I think. That would be old enough."

Nicholas assessed Jake. "I dunno, Sarah, that'd be a long time to wait. Jake's awful old."

Jake grunted. "This old man's ready for something to eat. You know how us *old* folks are. We get cranky if we're not fed on a regular basis."

"So do pit bulls." Sarah wrinkled her nose.

"And you know how dangerous they are when they're riled, don't you?" Jake noticed how Sarah's lips dented in when she tried to hold back her smile. Her lips had been silky warm. . . . He frowned. "Sit down and eat, Nicholas."

Nicholas giggled. "I didn't mean to hurt your feelings, Jake." He turned to Sarah. "When we going fishing?"

"Don't push it, sport." Jake cut Nicholas's sandwich into quarters.

"No, it's all right. I promised I'd take him. Just let me wake up a bit and we'll see what we need, okay?" She smiled when Nicholas looked relieved. "Were you worried?"

He chewed a nail. "Sometimes people forget promises. Jake doesn't, though."

Jake's hard face softened as he spoke to Nicholas. "Promises are important, kid. I told you that."

"Do you keep all your promises?" Sarah took out milk and a tall glass.

"I don't make promises." But of course he had. He'd promised to take care of Nicholas.

Sarah opened the silverware drawer and removed an iced tea spoon. She put the spoon in the glass and poured coffee in as she thought about Jake's comment. "You never make promises?"

He tilted his chair back. "Very seldom." He frowned as he watched her.

Sarah wondered if he remembered what he'd said before he sent her from the room. Hadn't that been a promise? "That's a hard way to live. People need promises and commitments from other people. They need to know they can count on each other.'' She added three spoonfuls of sugar to the hot coffee and then poured in cold milk to the top of the glass. Vigorously stirring, she sank into a chair.

''Most people make easy promises that aren't worth a hill of beans. So what difference does it make if I don't make any?''

''I'm not sure.'' She ran her finger around the chilled rim of her glass. Jake sounded annoyed. What kind of life had he had to make him so distrustful? Even in her darkest moments, she'd never been that cynical. ''Don't you get lonely?''

''No.'' But she noticed that his eyes slid to Nicholas.

''What happens when you do make promises?'' Sarah persisted, wanting to hear the words. She drank her iced coffee and watched as Jake chewed his sandwich.

''Then I keep them.'' He scowled and answered her question before she asked it. ''Always.''

''Then you're a person people can depend on.'' Sarah didn't like the shadow that moved over his face. He looked as though he wanted to argue but couldn't. She let him off the hook. ''That's enough serious talk for the morning, right, Nicholas? Don't you think we need to head out to the lake before the day gets away from us?''

''Yeah!'' Nicholas shoved his plate away and leaped up.

''Wait a minute. Sarah and I need to talk about some things first. Why don't you go outside and wait for us?''

The screen door thwacked behind Nicholas, and Sarah laughed just as Jake spoke. ''Maybe Nicholas and I should—''

''I know what you're going to say, but I've been thinking.'' Sarah leaned forward. ''I'd like for you and Nicholas to stay for a while. If you want to.''

His glance was wary.

Sarah hated her awkwardness, but she wasn't used to hiding her motives. Did he think she was making some kind of pass or something? She was attracted to him, but that wasn't why she wanted them to stay. "I mean, Nicholas is having such a good time and I like having him around." She tried to hide her embarrassment. "There's a wonderful festival coming up next week, Chalo Nitka. It's Seminole for 'big bass.' There's a midway, hay-diving, kids' games."

As Jake continued to stare at her, she grew more uncomfortable.

"I've been going since I was a kid. You know the Seminoles wrestle alligators." She realized she was babbling and didn't know how to stop.

"I don't think—" A false note twanged in his hesitation.

"If you're short of money or anything, well, you could help me out for a few days to pay for room and board," she interrupted. She'd have offered to let him stay for free, but she wasn't sure how he'd react. She didn't want him going off in a huff because she'd wounded his male pride.

Jake was caught between a rock and a hard place. Sarah's face glowed with excitement. He was in a no-win situation. He didn't want to leave Nicholas, but he didn't see how he could take him. He didn't know if he wanted to rip free of the delicate web Sarah was weaving around him, and he didn't even know if he could.

Sarah continued. "Stay for a week? You don't have to take Nicholas home yet, do you?"

The situation was almost funny. "No."

"Stay, then."

He wanted to.

"Pretty please with cream and sugar?" She tipped her head as she laughed self-consciously. "That's what we always said as kids. It usually worked."

Jake knew he shouldn't leave without knowing, really knowing, what kind of woman she was. He still had questions about her. It wasn't that he wanted to stay, not really. He ignored the little voice that told him he was lying. "Okay. We'll stay. I'm not short of money, but I'm not used to being waited on. You don't run a resort, so we'll help out. But just until Cholley Nitka—''

"Chalo Nitka."

"Whatever. Until then. Thanks." Jake picked up the plates. "Put me to work." Her smile was so warm and open he almost grabbed her and kissed her. He sighed. Staying was never going to work.

"Oh, c'mon," she teased. "It's not going to be that much work."

"The work's the least of it," he mumbled, thinking they were talking at cross-purposes.

Sunlight caught in the shining brown strands of her hair. "No?" For an instant he glimpsed awareness in her eyes, and then she withdrew. "Tell you what. I'll let you do the easy work—the dishes—while I get the boat ready. After all—you cooked, you need the rest."

Her face was smooth and soft and he wanted to touch her. "Did anyone ever tell you that you have a sassy mouth?" Jake scraped the garbage into a sack.

"Never!"

"Real sassy," he grumbled. "Going to get you in trouble one of these days," he added. He couldn't help looking at her sassy mouth.

"Promises, promises," she taunted and then blushed a brighter pink.

Jake was remembering, too. Remembering the ache he'd felt near her, remembering how he'd wanted her, remembering how he'd promised that it would be nice. That was a promise he couldn't afford to keep.

"So go on out before the kid makes himself dizzy enough to throw up. He runs in circles more than any living thing I ever saw." Jake opened the dishwasher. "Any tricks to this gizmo?"

"Nope." She looked back at him over her shoulder. The long line of her throat disappearing into her blouse led his eyes to her breasts. He saw her swallow before she looked away.

"Now you're starting to sound like me." If he couldn't control his thoughts any better than his eyes, he was in deep trouble.

"Yep." She laughed as she let the back door slam behind her. "Hey, Nicholas. Let's go down to the dock."

Jake watched her long legs eat up the distance between her and Nicholas. For a small woman, she had the longest legs. He couldn't turn away when he saw her arm go around Nicholas, who leaned against her.

Angrily Jake scraped and rinsed the rest of the dishes. Where was the little squirt's loyalty? Was he so hungry for a mother's love that he'd go to any female? Jake slammed the dishwasher door shut and locked it.

Hell. He'd forgotten the soap. He yanked the door open and dumped in the powder. What had made him agree to stay? Stupidity, that's what. He felt like pounding on something, preferably his own thick skull. In a silent stream of oaths garnered from dives and hellholes around the world, he cursed himself for being every kind of ass before he followed Sarah out the back door.

"Do you lock up around here?" he bellowed.

"I suppose you might as well since we'll be gone a while," Sarah called back. She and Nicholas were already in the bass boat. Engulfed in a fluorescent orange life vest, Nicholas was holding the tie-up rope in his hands while Sarah held on tightly to him.

Jake muttered under his breath and strode back to the house. A pit bull was just what he felt like. He'd like to chomp down on something and chew it to ribbons. What made him the angriest was that he couldn't figure out what was sticking in his craw so bad. Kids. Women. Who wanted them? Who needed them?

Sarah sat back near the motor and Jake put Nicholas on the middle seat and faced them. Mid-morning sun sparkled off the water as they headed away from land. Nicholas pointed his nose into the wind and Jake stretched his legs on either side of Nicholas, keeping him close.

"Faster, Sarah!" Nicholas's shriek whipped away from Jake.

"Okay, hang on!" Sarah sped up, but Jake noticed that she minimized bumps by keeping the boat angled to the chop.

The sun warmed the chill of the air and Jake leaned back, watching Nicholas enjoy the splashes of water and the boat ride. Sarah and Nicholas sported identical grins. The kid loved it. He'd love living here. Jake gritted his teeth.

They roared out and then circled over to a barely visible hammock. Egrets rose in a cloud around them.

She killed the motor and the boat silently settled into the water. Nicholas's eyes were huge and Sarah's face shone with joy.

Jake leaned back and shut his eyes against the sight of them together. Orange blossoms carried over the darker smell of the lake. Since they were sheltered from the wind by the hammock, the sun was hot. The peaceful rocking of the boat as the waves slapped it, and the woman and boy opposite him, filled up the world for Jake at that moment. He could almost put a name to the feelings tumbling inside him.

"C'mon, lazy bones." Sarah nudged his leg with her sneakered foot. "Wake up. I'm the one who should be falling asleep."

"Hush, woman, I'm busy doing man-type work."

"What's that," Sarah jeered, "sleeping?"

Her foot nudged him again, but he refused to open his eyes. The moment was too peaceful.

"Of course not. Man was made to decide the fate of the world. That kind of serious thinking requires elimination of all outside distractions." Jake folded his arms under his head. "And that's what I'm doing. Serious thinking."

"Okay, party pooper, I'd still call it sleeping, but Nicholas and I came to do some dedicated fishing. You stay here and solve the world's problems while we go wading."

The boat wobbled, and he heard a splash as they jumped into the water.

"You're not quite big enough to fish like this, Nicholas, but I think we can work out something. The vest will support you, and I can lift you when you cast. Your feet won't touch bottom, but you'll be okay. If it doesn't work, we'll go back to the boat and let you cast out of it."

"I'm not scared or anything, Sarah, but I just wondered if there might be alligators or something like that around here?"

Nicholas's voice had an edge of panic. Jake knew people fished out of the boats, and there were alligators in the lake. And water moccasins. His eyes snapped open and he sat up.

They were a few yards away from the anchored boat. Water sloshed up to Sarah's waist, and Nicholas bobbed on the rippled surface like an orange cork.

Jake's light-dazzled eyes saw a rounded, reptilian snout sliding off the hammock in their direction. He couldn't trust Sarah to save Nicholas. Lunging in their direction, he pitched himself into the water.

Chapter Six

Water splashed into Jake's face. With long, powerful reaches of his arms, he stroked quickly towards Sarah and Nicholas. Swimming was faster than slogging through the weed-clogged bottom. He didn't stop to think about Sarah's astonished yelp as he hauled Nicholas up with one arm and her with the other. He slung Nicholas into the safety of the boat and grabbed Sarah's blouse, throwing her bottom side up over into the boat.

The boat pitched wildly. Jake grabbed its sides. His face was beside Sarah's sopping green shorts and sleek legs as she turned to him. Wet, tanned skin glistened in front of his mouth as he hung onto the boat.

"What in heaven's name do you think you're doing?" She wiggled into the boat, tennis shoes spraying water into his eyes.

"This is fun, Jake! Let's do it again!" Nicholas scrambled to the side, ready to leap into the coffee-colored water.

"Sit down, Nicholas," Sarah said. She glanced at Jake. "I don't think Jake's playing games."

"Damn right I'm not!" Jake thumped into the boat. His heart was pumping full-tilt. He was as furious as he'd ever been in his life.

The explosion of his voice surprised him as much as it did Sarah. "What's the matter with you, getting out of the boat like that? What kind of guide dumps herself and a five-year-old kid in the middle of a snake-swarming, gator-infested lake? One big bull was swimming just over to the right of where you were! My God, what were you thinking of?" He shook water out of his hair and smashed it with shaking hands.

Nicholas's eyes were wide and he was chewing his finger-nails. Jake didn't want to scare the kid but, damn, Sarah should have had enough sense to stay in the boat. He should have said something himself. Fear still churned his blood.

Sarah's voice was very quiet. "Look around you, Jake. Tell me what you see."

Jake rubbed Nicholas's shoulder and looked back at the water. Ripples puckered the surface. A blue heron stalked at the edge of the hammock. Not far from the hammock, a brown-gray log swayed with the movement of water and breeze. A fish plopped fatly back under the light water slapping against the side of the gently moving boat. The log swayed again.

Jake looked at Sarah. "It looked like a gator."

"An easy mistake to make, but how could you think I'd put Nicholas in danger? What kind of person do you think I am?" Anger sharpened her voice.

She'd asked the unanswerable question. How could he tell her what kind of person he knew she was?

"I grew up on the lake!" she continued. "I've seen it low and dry, I've seen it when alligators were so scarce they were an endangered species. I know where they are. I know where it's safe to fish and where it's not! This is my living."

"Gators are all over the place! I saw them in the canals.
Didn't you just have an open-season hunt down here?"
Damned if he'd give an inch.

Very politely, Sarah answered. "There was a lottery for a
certain number of licenses. Yes, there are more gators
around than there used to be. People who live around here
know to be prudent. I live around here. I'm a prudent person." Sarcasm dripped from her voice.

He'd made a fool of himself.

Sarah knew it, too. Her raised eyebrows expressed her
wrath.

He'd been a jerk.

He fidgeted. Waited for heaven to rescue him. Stretched
and yawned. Fidgeted.

Sarah's lips twitched. Then a quiver moved across her
face like sun on water. He heard her giggle. What was so
funny? He hated giggling women.

An undignified snort escaped Sarah. "If you could have
seen yourself!"

"Yeah?" He shifted uncomfortably, energy still cours-
ing through him.

"You came barreling out of the boat like a cannonball! I
couldn't imagine what in the world was happening. And the
look on your face! You moved so fast and the next thing I
knew I was hanging face down in the boat. Not that I don't
appreciate the gesture, but the boat bottom stinks like fish
bait."

"Yeah, well, sorry." He started thinking about how he
must have looked thrashing towards her. "A moose in the
water, huh?"

She pulled her mouth together, but her eyes gave her
away. They sparkled. And then she lost it. "A whale!"
Whoops of laughter shook her. "I couldn't believe it! And
it was just a log!"

The joke had been on him, but she didn't have to be enjoying it so much. After all, he'd been worried about them.

Worried, hell. He'd been terrified. "You okay, sport?" Nicholas nodded.

But they were safe. That was the important thing, and a giggling Sarah was more appealing than was good for either one of them. Jake's adrenaline and fear found their own outlet. He needed to release his tension. He knew he shouldn't touch her, meant only to startle her a little.

He reached for one slim leg. "A whale? I think I've been insulted. Didn't you ever learn what happens when you don't pick on people your own size?" He pulled her inexorably toward him.

"Definitely a whale!" Sarah whooped again, helpless with laughter. "Oh, help!"

Jake snagged her other ankle. "A cannon, a whale. I get no respect, at all," he mourned, grasping her elbows. Her legs were tangled with his own densely muscled ones, and the slide of her skin against his thighs changed the game for him.

Her mouth opened slightly as she sensed his arousal. For one charged moment, she looked at him with such mischief and sweetness that his fingers clamped around her arms as desire stirred. He'd meant to keep the mood light. She pivoted, and her knee slipped inside his legs. The brush of her soft skin against his burned.

"Turn me loose," she laughed, "or you'll be sorry. I was wrestling champ in fourth grade!"

"This isn't fourth grade, sweetheart. And I've been out of school a long time."

Her laughing face was shiny pink.

Nicholas leaped into the fray and the boat wobbled. "I'll help you, Sarah!" He swatted Jake.

"Cry uncle?" Jake murmured.

"I'm not afraid of you," Sarah scoffed.

"Maybe you should be." He wanted her afraid of him so he could remember how treacherous she was, not warm and funny like this, bewitching him.

"You're all bark, no bite. Or should I go for a *whale* of a comparison?" She laughed again, but then he slid his palm under her calf and pulled her closer. Her eyes darkened.

Jake gathered Sarah to him with one arm and fended off Nicholas, who was butting him in the chest, with the other. "No fair ganging up. One on one is the rule, right, Sarah?" Around her waist, his fingers brushed a damp curve. He wanted to leave his hand there. His arm tensed.

"Uncle," Sarah whispered, no dummy.

Her mouth trembled. Jake wanted to touch it, but instead he grabbed Nicholas up and dangled him over the water.

"Help, Sarah!" Nicholas shrieked. "Jake's gonna throw me to the sharks and stuff!" Delightedly screeching, he wriggled in Jake's secure grasp.

Sarah pulled at Jake's arm and pushed him backward.

"I thought you said 'uncle'?" He let her press her slim hands against him and yielded. As Sarah fell on top of him, Jake hauled Nicholas in close. Two pairs of identical blue eyes gleamed roguishly at him. One softly rounded chin and one pointy one dug into his chest as mother and son observed him. For a long moment he watched them, and his heart turned over.

"I lied," Sarah teased.

That was the problem. Clutching Sarah and Nicholas, Jake finally identified the aching pain in the vicinity of his ungovernable heart. He couldn't trust her, but he kept wanting her. He wanted her and liked her, and didn't trust her. Yet he wanted to stay here with both of them wrapped in his arms. He grimaced.

"You got a stummick ache?" Nicholas patted Jake's belly sympathetically.

"No, sport, not a stomach ache."

Sarah rubbed Jake's chin. "Poor old Jake. He's not as fierce as he pretends."

Her smile gently mocked him. She'd seen his confusion. What would she do if he told her everything? Could he trust her explanations?

He stared at her, wondering what she was thinking as she watched him so solemnly. He'd like making love with Sarah Jane Simpson, watching her unfold bit by bit. Her breasts moved against him as she breathed, a sweet weight that curled his insides into knots of yearning.

"Jake?"

He might not be able to make her fall in love with him, but she wasn't indifferent to him—that was for sure. He could turn that against her, trap her. He could bind her to him with the chains of her own needs. And then she couldn't kick him out. Wouldn't want to. Then he'd know the truth about her.

"Yes, Sarah?" His arms anchored her to him.

"This isn't recommended boating procedure." She levered upright against him. "Come on back to your seat, Nicholas, and let's see if we can retrieve our dignity, okay?"

Nicholas frowned.

Jake frowned.

"Dinity's not as much fun." Nicholas plunked his behind on the seat and folded his arms, a miniature Jake.

The gesture absurdly touched Jake.

"But safer." Sarah crawled back to her seat near the Johnson motor. "So, fellas, what now? Any suggestions?"

"I didn't catch a fish."

"True," Sarah admitted. "I said we'd go fishing, and I guess it doesn't count if you don't catch a fish."

Nicholas nodded hopefully.

"What do you think, Moby Dick?" Sarah nudged Jake with her wet sneaker.

Every time she touched him, she sent tiny firecrackers along his skin. Bing. Bing. Bing.

"Think you could handle some more serious thinking while we see what's biting? We'll stay in the boat with you," she teased. "We'd hate to interrupt your 'man's work' with an unscheduled swim."

"Nobody appreciates a hero anymore," Jake grumbled. "Sure, go ahead and fish to your heart's content. Don't mind me. I'll just stretch out here and if I get in the way, just heave me over the side."

"You are so silly, Jake." Nicholas shook his head. "We wouldn't throw you to the sharks. You know that."

"Besides," Sarah added gravely, "there aren't any sharks in the lake." She nodded at Nicholas's disappointed expression.

"No sharks? Well, damn—"

"Nicholas!" Jake roared.

"Sorry, Jake. I been trying to remember. But it's a, a danged shame, that's what. There should be sharks. That'd be real neat."

Nicholas was clearly miffed by the lost opportunity to feed something, if not Jake, to the sharks. Bloodthirsty little monster. Jake sighed. Kid was going to be a pistol when he grew up. Be nice to see it happen.

"We can always chop off Jake's toes and use them for fish bait if we need to," Sarah consoled.

For a moment Jake thought Nicholas was considering it.

Nicholas shook his head. "Better not, Sarah." To his credit, he looked a little worried as he reassured Jake. "Sarah's just kidding you, Jake. She wouldn't do that. Anyway, we got lots of bait."

"Terrific, kid." Jake stretched out once again and wondered what disaster was next. "Fish away, but leave my toes alone."

Through partially closed eyes, he watched Sarah and Nicholas. The sun was drying her pink blouse in patches, leaving intriguing places damp and clinging. He'd like to slide his finger in under the damp spots and lift them up to dry. Her skin would be water-chilled and then warm quickly. There was one spot just at the side of her left breast that was particularly slow to dry. That was his favorite spot. The curve of her breast shaped the damp material and he could see through the thin material.

"Here, Nicholas, use your wrist like this to pop the lure over the water."

Sarah's arm lifted up, and the damp material tightened against her lifted breast. That spot was beginning to obsess him. If he were lucky, it would dry fast. If he were luckier, it wouldn't.

She looked at him just then under her upraised arm and once again her face picked up the pink of her blouse. He smiled, a long, slow smile that let her know he liked what he saw, a smile that told her he'd like to do more than look. Her face flushed brighter pink.

Jake liked the way she hurried into speech. He watched her lips move with the syllables and wanted to feel their texture under his fingers, under his own lips. There was no other solution. He was going to have to lure Sarah Jane Simpson into betraying the truth. Lulled into trusting him she'd make a mistake sooner or later. He was doing the right thing for Nicholas. Jake smiled with satisfaction even as uneasiness about his own motives flickered.

"Nicholas, give the lure a little lift every now and then. Make it look real."

Real. That was how life would be every day if Sarah and Nicholas were always around him. The three of them, fishing, joking. Loving. The mirage shimmered in the sun, wrapping him in its warmth, seductive.

Laziness curled around him and carried him along in its slow drifting current. He lay there, lulled by warmth and peace, and watched Sarah with her son.

"Nicholas, we're going to move to a different spot and try some shiners. Maybe they'll work today." Sarah fired the engine and guided the boat away from the lee of the hammock out into the wind.

The choppier water spanked the boat bottom and wrenched Jake out of his sleepy indolence. "Want me to work the motor?"

"Oh, sure," Sarah gibed. "Insult my competence, make me say 'uncle,' and now you want to play captain. Fat chance." She stuck out her tongue.

Nicholas's mouth dropped open. "That's rude, Sarah." He turned to Jake. "Isn't it?"

"Yep. But," Jake leaned over, "it's just as rude to tell her." He winked at Nicholas.

"Oh." Nicholas cocked his head at Jake. "So when I stick out my tongue, you'll be rude if you yell at me?"

The boat hit a wave hard. Jake heard Sarah's stifled laughter. "Uh, not quite that way, sport. Anyway, Sarah was teasing." He wished her laugh didn't fizz inside him.

"I sure don't understand this teasing stuff," Nicholas moaned. "How come when I tell you I didn't do something I did do and then I say I'm teasing, you still yell?" He jammed his elbows on his knees. "Don't seem fair."

"No, I guess not." Jake gave up. He was fresh out of answers. The kid had more unanswerable questions than space.

"Nicholas, hand me the bait bucket, please." Sarah splashed the anchor over.

"What are we gonna do with the little fishies?" Anxiety crept into his voice.

Jake chuckled. He knew what was coming. Sarah couldn't handle this one.

"We're going to fish with them. Here, just hold it right behind the fin."

Through his lashes, Jake watched Nicholas reach out carefully with cupped hands.

"They tickle."

"Be careful and don't let it slip out, now." The bucket lid clanged shut. "I'll put mine on the hook and then you'll see how it's done." She hesitated, and a frown pleated her forehead. "What's the matter?"

"Nothin'."

Moving slightly so that the sun wasn't blinding him, Jake played possum, waiting for Sarah to fail.

"Okay, then," Sarah continued. "Just slip the hook gently in all the way through and then, very carefully now, use your wrist to flick the line out, just the way you did with the lures." The boat rocked as Sarah edged closer to Nicholas. "Got it?"

"The doctor gave me shots. With a needle."

"Oh?"

"That was a little needle and it hurt."

"Yes?" Sarah's voice was patient.

She wasn't hurrying the kid or rushing him to get back to the business at hand.

Idly, Jake wondered what kind of lover she'd be. If he knew anything about women—and a life spent on the fringes had taught him a lot, he reckoned—Sarah wouldn't be a passive lover, content to let someone else establish the pace. She would be involved wholeheartedly. Body, heart and soul, she would lose herself in the act and the man. He pushed the deceptive image away.

"This is a big hook, Sarah."

"So it is."

She was quicker than he would have been, Jake had to admit.

"Awful big." Stubbornness settled into Nicholas's voice.

"You know, Nicholas, I've been thinking. The lures are so pretty when they flash out to the water. I'd almost rather use them. Would you mind?"

"No. But what're you gonna do with the little fishies?"

"Gosh, I just don't know." Sarah sighed. "Do you have any ideas?"

"I liked swimming in the lake."

"I did, too." Silence.

"It's a big lake."

"Sure is. Over seven hundred square miles, as a matter of fact."

Hell, she was smooth. Her earnestness almost convinced him.

"These fishies would like swimming here, I think."

"Me, too, honey. Why don't we let them go for it?"

Nicholas squealed as he slipped his hands into the water. "Look at my guy go! Hurry up with the others. They're missing the fun."

Sarah kneeled at the edge of the boat, slowly lowering the bait bucket into the water. Against the sun, her small figure was a curving, dark shadow making Jake hunger for night and Sarah all to himself on her pale sheets in a quiet room. Her shadow, his, blending in the musky night.

"There they go. They've all swum out."

"Hey, Jake, look at 'em!"

Summoned to the party, Jake roused himself to lean over the side. The shiners moved this way, that, quick patterns of silver in dark water.

"Real pretty, kid." Jake's arm lay close to Sarah's. Her slender bones felt fragile.

Her smile flashed like the minnows as she hauled the bucket back. "So much for reality. Let's head in."

When they docked, Nicholas headed away with his fishing rod while Sarah reached into the bait well to drain it. When she looked towards the house, Nicholas was disappearing around the corner, out of sight and sound.

She straightened up, her fingers dripping water on Jake's leg. Very deliberately, with all the tenderness at his skill, he turned her wet hand wrist side up and placed his index finger on the pulse point, lightly holding her captive. "You're very good with him."

"I like him." Under his touch her pulse was a tiny trip-hammer.

"I can see that." Jake scraped his fingernail slightly against her skin as he moved his finger slowly up to the bend of her elbow where the blue veins showed. He wanted to be slow and easy with her, gentle, despite all he suspected.

She shivered. "What are you doing?"

"Why, Miss Simpson, don't you know?" Jake teased her as his finger edged softly up to the inside of her arm. Her mouth was slightly parted as she watched his face.

"No," she breathed. "I haven't the foggiest idea. Why don't you tell me?"

"Shame on you, Miss Sarah Jane. Don't you recognize a courting gentleman when you see one?"

Her breath was cinnamon sweet. Jake smiled as he leaned down and kissed the end of her pink nose. "I'm courting you, sweet Sarah, that's what I'm doing." The words sounded so right and the touch of her tempted him to forget the role he was playing.

Sarah looked at him as though he were speaking in tongues. "You've been in the sun too long. It's baked your brains," she sputtered, at a loss.

Sure, her first response had been an eager curling up of every nerve ending, but that was just hormones, and she already knew the effect Jake had on her treacherous hormones. Not to mention the hungry-outlaw look in his eyes, which undermined her emotions. She didn't have any defense against that loneliness.

"Think so?" He took her hand and laid it against his forehead. Water dripped down her wrist. "Want to check for fever?" He slid her wrist down against his chin. "See? No fever."

Her temperature shot up several degrees.

"Prepare yourself, Sarah. I'm in a flowers-and-candy, sitting-on-the-front-porch-courting frame of mind." The lethal toughness of Jake's craggy face softened.

Liquid sunshine flowed through her veins. "I'm not sure I'm ready for courting."

"What do you have to do to get ready? Iron your frilly white blouse? Oil the squeaky porch swing?"

"I don't know. I don't think I've ever been courted before." His thumb moved to her neck, which arched before she could stop it.

"So get your iron and oil can out because you're going to be courted, sweetheart."

"I don't have any frilly white blouses." Her neck curved into his relentlessly tracing thumb which glided down to her collarbone and flipped the button there back and forth.

"This blouse isn't bad. I think I could court you very easily while you're wearing it." His smile hinted that maybe he could court her better if she weren't wearing it, at all.

Sarah went hot from scalp to toe. "You're not the courting type."

"That's true," he mused, "but somehow with you, sweetheart, I think I could be." The reluctant note of truth in his voice weakened her knees, knees that had been churned to butter since his first words. "I was never interested in courting before."

"Why now?" She had to know. He'd come out of the dark and insinuated himself into her life and there were unanswered questions in spite of the sizzle between them.

"You."

Sarah heard Nicholas splashing in the empty bait wells. She looked down at Jake's fingers. She remembered how they had looked clasped around her front door. Even then she had noticed them, their strength and control.

"What about me?" She asked.

"You—make me begrudge all my wasted years." He added as she frowned, "Years lost passing time in smoky places where dreams hung in the air and drifted out the open windows. Places where people come when they have nowhere else to go. I want somewhere to go, Sarah. I want someone to come home to."

Sarah wanted to weep at the emptiness in Jake's voice. What kind of loneliness had eaten away at his soul? No wonder he'd become so attached to Nicholas. Jake's rough prickliness was his defense against a world in which he had no home.

She reached out her hand to touch his cheek. "I don't know what to say."

"Don't say anything, then." He pressed his fingers to her lips. "Just give me time. Let me," he paused, as though searching for the right word, "let me court you."

Urgency came at her in waves. "An odd choice of words, Jake. What, exactly, do you want from me?"

Jake's hand pressed hers tightly to his face, holding it as if it were a lifeline. "Everything, Sarah, everything you have to give. I want it all."

She'd seen him with Nicholas, seen his emptiness, and couldn't turn away despite her doubts. "I'm not sure we're even talking about the same things. You disturb me. Yes," she added as he leaned forward, "I know you've made me feel something I never thought to feel, never hoped to feel." She cradled his face between her hands. "But that's not enough. I'm not sure what you're after." Releasing him, she held up her empty hands.

"Haven't you been listening?" His palm cupped the back of her head, rubbed the taut muscles of her neck. "Permanence is what I'm after. Nothing less. That's what this is all about."

She moved uneasily. "You don't understand."

"Then make me." He slipped his hand down the back of the blouse, comforting, caressing with slow sweeps of his callused palm.

She wanted to tell him how empty her life had been until he and Nicholas stormed in, shattering her defenses, but that was a risk she wasn't prepared to take. She was too raw and Jake was moving too fast.

"Come on, sweetheart, tell me," he encouraged. "We
have to start somewhere, and the first step is the hardest.
You took it last night when you talked to me. What can be
so hard about the next step?"

"So much pain." Her voice sank. "I don't want to feel
that much pain ever again in my life."

He wrapped both arms around her. "Pain's not what it's
about, sweetheart. I would never cause you pain."

She freed herself. "You couldn't keep from it. Pain's part
of living." Sarah heard herself. For the first time she'd put
it into words. That was what she feared—pain. And she was
right. Pain was a part of life. Cutting away pain had cut her
off from life. "I'm a coward," she said and knew it was
true.

"Never, not you, my tiger with a baseball bat." His voice
puffed the strands of her hair and tickled her earlobe. "Give
me time, Sarah."

"How much?" She'd known she wasn't ready for the
need she'd sensed in Jake, but she hadn't thought events
would spiral out of control this way. She wanted to give Jake
the time he asked, but she was terrified. "How much?" she
repeated insistently, hoping he'd force her into a corner and
she'd have to—have to what?

"As much time as it takes." His voice was flat.

"That's ridiculous. You must have a job—I don't even
know what your job is," she protested. "This is impossible." She twisted away from him.

"Sarah?" Jake touched her and his eyes narrowed as
though he'd seen something unexpected in her face.

Sarah welcomed Nicholas's interruption.

"Jake, I got an owie," Nicholas whimpered.

"How'd you do that, sport?" Jake looked at the hook
lodged through Nicholas's forearm. "Da—Hurts like a son
of a gun, I'll bet, huh?" he said as Nicholas's whimper
turned to a full-fledged yowl. "Just hang on, we'll have it
out in a minute."

Jake's color faded to a sickly brown when he examined the hook piercing the thin arm, and perspiration soaked his dark hair. He wiped the sweat off his face with the back of his arm. "Do you have any pliers?"

Sarah felt the faint tremor as he took the pliers. She knew, as Jake did and couldn't face, that Nicholas was going to hurt more before the hook was out. The barbs lodged in the flesh were going to have to come out one way or another, and Nicholas was ready to pitch into hysterical tears.

"Want me to do it, Nicholas, while Jake holds your arm steady? Jake's so strong that I think he'll steady you better than I could." Sarah kept looking right at Nicholas and talking to him in a low voice. The rapidity with which Jake slapped the pliers into her palm told her of his relief.

Sarah rubbed her nose as she looked into Nicholas's woebegone face. She wished she hadn't volunteered, but she'd had no choice. They'd needed her. She wanted to tuck Nicholas's hair behind his funny little ears.

"I won't lie to you, Nicholas. This will hurt. You can handle it, though, okay?" Sarah turned his arm towards Jake and gestured for Jake to hold it so that Nicholas could see. "I'm not going to hide anything from you, honey, and we're going to work really fast so that it won't hurt long. You can help."

"What 'cha want me to do?" he bawled, tears raining down his cheeks, "'cause it hurts like hell." His small mouth was screwed up as he tried to keep the sobs inside.

"Oh, sugar, I know it does. It's going to be better in just a minute, though." Sarah wanted to bawl herself. "Now listen, I think you'll want to watch so that you can tell everybody how brave you were. And I want you to raise your other hand if I'm making it worse, okay? Can you do that?" Sarah smoothed his hair away from his forehead and kissed him. Fishy and sweaty, he leaned against her and she ached to draw him closer.

"Sure," he gulped.

"I also need your help with Jake." Sarah worked quickly to snip off the line from the eye of the hook, leaving the barbs still buried. Fashioning a loop out of the fish line, she took the loop and slid it between the shank of the hook and Nicholas's skin up to the bend of the hook.

"What do you want me to do with Jake?" Nicholas turned his head just as Sarah slipped the loop around the curve.

"Well, you know how tough guys are. Sometimes you have to watch them. A lot of times they faint." Sarah kept talking as fast as she could while she worked.

"Not Jake," Nicholas insisted through his tears, clearly astonished that Sarah could suggest such a thing.

"Probably not, but keep an eye on him for me, will you?"

Nicholas fixed his eyes on Jake.

"I'd sure hate to have to fish him out of the lake." Sarah pressed her index finger against the eye of the hook, holding it firmly against Nicholas's skin as she snapped the metal shaft back out its entry point with a clean movement of her left hand that sent the hook sparkling into the water.

Just as she pulled on the shaft, Jake, with a quick look at her, flopped onto the dock.

"Sarah! Jake fainted!" Nicholas squirmed, his injury forgotten.

"Really?" Sarah gave Nicholas a big kiss and hug before turning him loose. Her hands were shaking.

Nicholas scrunched down and lifted Jake's eyelid.

"How's your owie, sport?" Jake sat up. A thin, white line outlined his hard mouth.

"You teasing me again, Jake? Or did you truly faint?" At Jake's wink, Nicholas sniffed, "I don't like this teasing stuff. And anyway, when you gonna take out this damn hook?"

When Sarah and Jake burst out laughing, Nicholas frowned. "What's so funny?"

As Sarah took Nicholas's hand, Jake reached to him. Their three hands met, Jake's broad and dark, hers slim and tanned, both protectively tented over Nicholas's grubby little fist.

Jake's somber gaze met hers. "Sarah—"

"Yes?" She waited.

"Nothing. Nothing, at all." Jake's cheek brushed Nicholas's forehead, a swift gesture. Holding Nicholas, Jake leaned over, kissing her hard on the lips, a puzzling, angry touch that melted her bones.

Chapter Seven

So Jake began his uneasy courting of Sarah.

The days were ruled by blue skies and sunny days, Jake's nights by doubt and longing.

Sarah said now that it was warm, they could go fishing for shell crackers. Wearing his bandage like a badge of honor, Nicholas allowed as how he wasn't sure he wanted to fish anymore. As for Jake, he was going crazier by the minute.

He tried to convince himself that the storm clouds on the horizon would blow past, but he was edgy and touchy. Tension rode him with roweled spurs.

He told himself that he had no choice, but he remembered all the times in his life when things had gone wrong—and the stakes had never been this high.

He chewed antacids by the handful, hoping the clawing in his gut would ease. It didn't.

He tried to stay away from Nicholas. He couldn't.

He tried to keep his hands and mouth off Sarah. He didn't.

He reminded himself by the hour that she was the enemy, but he couldn't be near her without wrapping his arms around her, pressing her up against a wall, a door, anything, and kissing her until his breath labored and his blood beat hard and thick.

She danced before him in butterfly colors, trailing wisps of green and yellow and pink in her wake, tossing shy smiles in his direction before hurrying off and taking all the color with her.

One day he found himself in her bedroom breathing in the scent she'd left behind. Dust motes danced near the window. Her dresser was tidy, but the essence of Sarah lingered, and he gripped her cotton nightgown hanging on the back of the door until his fingers cramped.

The false days crept by for Jake and his role became terrifyingly comfortable. He found himself trying to surprise those throaty, little laughs from her and knew something had to break soon. He hoped it wouldn't be him. He wanted Sarah anywhere, everywhere. He wanted her bound to him, so bound that he could break her and free himself.

Yet in the still of the night, as Nicholas slept in the bed across from him, a nasty little voice kept Jake awake. "Yeah, you're responsible for Nicholas, but you want her, too. That's why you're staying. Who're you kidding, chump?"

Waking up tired and frustrated, Jake crawled out of his twisted sheets and forced himself through days where he swung between go and stay, anger and desire.

Today was no different, he thought sourly as he scraped leaves into a pile. Nicholas had gone off with Sarah's cousin Buck, and Jake couldn't forget for a second that he and Sarah were alone. He was keeping as firm a grip on his hunger as he was on the rake he worked so ruthlessly through the grass.

Sarah opened the screen door. "What's this?" She thrust the lumpy package she'd found on the kitchen table toward

Jake. Looking up at her, he shaded his face, and she let her eyes linger on the muscles outlined by his close-fitting T-shirt, let them drift down over the sprung-hip stance that pulled his jeans tight over his pelvis.

Large and solid, he moved towards her, first leaning the rake against the oak. "A present." His grin was sly, and her breathing quickened at his look.

"You shouldn't have!" She traced the knobbly outlines of the brown-papered present.

"You're right. I shouldn't have." He came close, walking right into her space, surrounding her with him, sliding his big palms over her shoulders and down her back, swooping them over her hips, her thighs, and inching up her rib cage, teasing and coaxing, making her quiver with the slightest skimming graze of his fingers or lips. She vibrated to his presence like a tuning fork.

He'd been doing that for the last two weeks. Imprinting her with himself until she craved the sight and touch of him.

"So why did you?" Sarah brandished the package at him and pushed her hair back from her ear.

"Um, much better." Jake nibbled on its outer curve.

The flick of his tongue against her skin turned her to hot butter. If he were toast, she'd be sliding all over him in a golden, melted flow.

"Jake." She turned her lips to him. His taste had become as necessary to her as breathing, the hot, male taste of arousal that told her how much he wanted her. A taste, too, of disquieting hostility.

Even so, Sarah slanted her lips to his, answering the urging of his lips and seeking tongue.

Jake's mouth consumed her, heat on heat, burning her to a crisp. He lifted her off her feet, pulling her to him. All along the length of his body, his strength and hardness supported and seduced her. Frantically she moved her head, moved against him. Need coiled and twisted inside her and the key was Jake.

The package thudded to the wooden planks, bounced.

"Hell." Carefully Jake let her slide down his length, and she burned, burned against him. He settled her against him while their breathing slowed.

Sarah leaned on him and pressed her lips to the black hair that curled over the neck of his white T-shirt. He smelled so good.

"Don't," he muttered, pulling her tight to him.

She blew gently into the black curls and heard his heart thunder under her ears in response. "Why not?" she murmured, knowing, but unable to resist the temptation of her senses.

"I'm trying to do this right. Give me some help."

"You're doing everything perfectly. Don't stop." She burrowed her nose where the strong muscles of his neck met his broad shoulders. She turned, pressing her lips to him, biting lightly at the rugged strength, tracing the tendons with her mouth.

His shudder resonated through her.

"Want me to stop?" she whispered.

"Hell, no. Yes." He swayed with her for a moment before pulling her against him as he leaned on the door. His sigh was heavy. "No wonder courting went out of style. Too hard on the nerves."

She laughed up at him. "But you have nerves of steel, hero man."

Sarah smoothed the dark circles under his eyes. The situation was explosive and until today she'd been avoiding him when she could. "You're not sleeping well."

"You got that right." At her murmured regret, he snacked on her nose. "It's all right. I'll survive. Maybe," he added as she slipped her arms around his neck. "Take a look at your present." He bent and picked it up. His smile was hesitant as he handed her the bumpy package, almost as though he were as surprised by the present as she.

"You're really taking this courtship seriously, aren't you?" She peeled back paper from the top.

"I'm very serious." He lifted her chin, forcing her to meet his eyes where emotions warred.

"I know." Yes, he was serious, but something was cracking him apart. Every time he was near her he gave off an air of desperation that troubled her and kept her from completely surrendering to the power he increasingly wielded over her senses.

She wished she could read him as clearly as he read her. One week had stretched into two, the weeks carving new grooves in his weathered face. He was a man in torment and it showed.

"I know," she repeated in an effort to ease the turmoil she sensed. She stood on tiptoe and kissed him, letting her lips linger against his, giving whatever comfort she could. "Now let's see this present." She stripped away a swath of paper. "What in the world?" She flourished a bright red can of WD-40 oil.

"I have plans." He shifted uncomfortably.

"A porch swing." She'd never suspected a sense of whimsy hid underneath Jake's roughness. Flirting, she stroked his chin with the can. "In the meantime, what about making use of the swing on the tree?" She quirked an eyebrow at him. "It tilts, though."

"Appropriate. That's how I feel every time I'm around you. Like the whole damn world has tilted and I'm sliding off the edge." His words sounded torn from him as he grabbed her arm and the WD-40 cartwheeled to the floor. "C'mere."

Curled on his lap in the swing with her arms around Jake's neck, Sarah tried to think of a way to continue a discussion begun two nights earlier and stonewalled by Jake. "We have to pick up Nicholas and head over to the Chalo Nitka pavilion. You don't mind that he went off with Buck, do you?" She finger-walked under Jake's shirt over to the spot on his ribs that he found so fascinating on hers.

"No. Of course not."

She heard the reserve. "Do you miss not having any family?"

"You don't miss what you don't know." He pushed against the ground, and his thighs moved under hers.

"You never found out why your mom left you?"

"It's not important. I made out okay." He dug his heels in the sand and slowed them. Bitterness echoed in his voice.

"How old were you?"

"Hell, I don't know. Nicholas's age, maybe seven."

"I see." That explained a lot.

He frowned at her. "There's nothing to see. I said it wasn't important."

"Of course not." Sarah could work out for herself how a six-year-old boy must have felt. "And later you lived with—?"

"Relatives." Off-limits signs sprang up around his clipped words.

Sarah wouldn't give up. "Until—?"

His muscles tensed under his shirt. "Look, in a nutshell, here it is. I ran away, joined the army, and I've been working as a consulting engineer for most of my life. The army's been my home. Okay?"

"Where did you work?"

"Here, there. Who cares? I work hard, I earn good money, I pay my taxes. Okay?"

Jake didn't go in for details.

"Poor Jake," she crooned, tiptoeing her fingers up his spine. His rough hand was sliding up and over her bare knee.

"Poor Jake, nothing. It's not your pity I crave at night when I'm lying there looking at the ceiling." He traced a circle on the underside of her knee.

Sarah stroked his back with the lightest of touches and changed the subject. "Do you think Nicholas is going to enjoy the small-fry fishing contest? He didn't have to fish."

Jake pumped the swing high. "He wants to do everything. Nonstop. All day."

"Buck's a wild man. Nicholas will be crazy about him. Actually," she mused, "he reminds me of Buck in some ways, same energy, I guess."

Jake moved suddenly, leaving her breathless. "I don't want to talk about your cousin," he breathed into her mouth, his tongue outlining her lips. "I've got better things to do with your mouth."

He curled his tongue around hers and chased all thoughts from her head.

She strained against him, wanting more than he was giving her, wanting something she sensed just over the horizon. Gripping Jake's face, she rained kisses all over his face, straining past the barriers she sensed in him, needing to comfort the child he'd been. "Jake," she whispered against his skin, "Oh, Jake."

The swing swooped up and out and her legs entwined with his and she felt him beneath her.

"Sarah, sweetheart, stop. This isn't working." Jake slowed the swing.

She moved against him. "Oh, I don't know. Seems to be working," she kidded.

He groaned. "Yeah, that's the problem."

"Or your solution?" The words popped out.

He stood up, supporting her until her feet touched the ground. "It's not like that."

"No?" Embarrassed but determined to have her say, Sarah ploughed on. "It seems to me that you use the attraction between us to avoid discussing issues. I'm not trying to pin you down, Jake, but I need to know what's happening with us because it's not like anything I've ever known." Miserable, she creased the front of her shorts.

He turned away from her and folded his arms. "I told you my intentions. You know what they are." When he looked at her again, the walls were up.

This was the Jake that kept her off balance.

"A courtship."

"A courtship," he concurred, glancing away.

"To what end?" The mockingbird in the xoria bush whistled its echo.

He shrugged. "I don't know." His cheekbones were a knife edge in the grooves of his face.

"But what do you want me to *do*?"

"Nothing."

Sarah held her hands out to him in supplication. She needed words from him, words she could build on, she realized in surprise.

She wanted to build on the feelings Jake had freed in her. Unnamed and unidentified, as they were, she wanted them to grow and flower into—whatever. Something. But a plant couldn't grow without nourishment, and chemistry wasn't nourishment enough.

"Sarah, don't look at me like that." Jake groaned and folded her in his arms. Against her, his heart beat steadily and surely.

There, held close to his heart, warmed by him, she was answered by his body in an old and wordless language until a cloud passing over the sun chilled her.

"We'd better go get Nicholas," she murmured, rubbing the goose bumps on her arm.

Jake's finger trailed down her arm, but he released her. "Yes." He looked up at the sky for a long time. "Let's go get Nicholas."

Bumping out of the driveway, they headed towards Moore Haven in silence.

Jake drummed a rhythm on the dashboard of his truck. *Sarah, what are you doing to me?*

Sarah tucked her knees under her and looked at the hyacinths in the ditches.

I like you, Jake Donnelly, but I don't trust the way you make me feel.

Jake twitched on the radio. A melancholy song filled the truck.

Oh, Sarah, if you were only what you seem to be.

Sarah glanced at Jake's hand on the dial as the words of the song plucked at her. "No, leave it on," she said as Jake started to turn off the radio. His eyes were hooded and she looked away.

Where's it all going to end, Jake?

When the song's notes died away, Sarah swallowed the lump in her throat.

"Where to?" Jake's words cut the silence.

"Highway 27, past the park and down to the river. The kids will be fishing south of the city docks. That's where the trophy tables are set up." Sarah fiddled with the door handle. "I wonder how Nicholas did."

"If he fished."

Jake slowed when they passed the new Chalo Nitka Park. People in bright plaid shirts and jeans, in Seminole traditional dress and in comfortable gear migrated in a kaleidoscope of color. "Those booths look like the Seminole 'chickees.'"

"They're modeled after the traditional homes. The floats and cars in the parade will have palm branches tied around them. Even the food will reflect Indian life. Want to try some swamp cabbage?" She relaxed as they resumed the more or less comfortable relationship that they'd fallen into before today.

Jake signaled a turn with his arm out the window. "I've eaten worse."

"It's like a potato with crunch." She laughed, glad he was picking up the mood.

"How're you going to cook it?"

"How do you feel about nouvelle cuisine?"

"Come again?" He switched off the engine.

"Thinly sliced swamp cabbage with a sprinkling of sea salt served over lightly grilled Okeechobee cat?"

"You're kidding, right? No?"

"Relax, Donnelly. I'll spare you the nouvelle, but you'll enjoy the rest of it, fried cat, raw or boiled swamp cabbage." Sarah grinned at him and stuck her feet up on the rusty dash. "Speaking of nouvelle, this truck could use some saucing up."

"It runs."

"Barely."

"Never, ever, insult a man's wheels, sweetheart," Jake growled, reaching his hand over and pulling her closer to him.

"That's about all this is. Wheels, antenna, brakes—it has brakes?" Sarah asked, alarmed.

"I don't know. I just let it run till it's out of gas and then I stop where it does."

"You said you'd made money consulting, so why this— uh, this—very interesting vehicle?" Sarah surveyed the interior of the cab with a wrinkled nose.

Springs coiled out of slits in the vinyl seats. Corroded bolts and hinges merrily flaked rust with each bouncing jolt. Wires draped in a decorative festoon under the dash.

"It's hard to explain."

"I'll just bet." She loved teasing him. She thought he'd probably seen little of the lighthearted side of life. "Kidding aside, Jake, how did you wind up with this antique? Not that it doesn't have character."

"I'd just gotten back from a job, I was in a hurry, it was late at night, and nothing much was open. I didn't have much cash in my pocket, so that's why this rolling wreck." He patted the steering wheel affectionately. "I'm starting to like the old girl. She grows on you."

"That I believe," Sarah said mournfully as she un-snagged her shorts from a roaming spring coil. "I wish this classic rust bucket had seat belts, though."

"Beggars can't be choosers. The three of us would never have fit in your windup toy."

"You mean *you* wouldn't have fit."

Jake wrapped his fingers around her knee and laughed. "Yeah, I thought I was going to be shifting my toes when I drove it. How far do I go?"

Sarah's knee was liquefying where his palm cupped it. How could she be so susceptible to his every touch? "Past the post office at First Street, until you start seeing crowds." She lifted his hand up and thumped it on his own knee.

He slanted a look. "Like that, huh?"

"You need both hands to drive this gem," Sarah declared and folded her hands primly in her lap. It would do him good to suffer a little. Of course, she thought gloomily, missing his warm grip, she was suffering, too.

"Damnation," Jake burst out as they pulled off the road. "Is every kid in Florida here?"

All up and down the banks of the Caloosahatchie, kids stretched in a long line. Sarah watched Jake's face as he searched for Nicholas. Jake didn't know it, maybe couldn't admit it, but he loved the child. Every anxious turn of his head betrayed him. Finally, he rubbed his neck and turned to her.

"How are we going to find him?"

"Easy," she said in a superior tone. "We'll find Buck."

"That's going to be easy?" Jake surveyed the elbow-to-elbow mass and throngs of children screaming around tables set up with rows of trophies.

"If you know what you're doing," she said smugly, taking his arm. "Remember, I'm the guide in these parts."

"I'm not proud. Lead on." He tucked his arm under hers.

Sarah wondered if he'd intentionally made sure his forearm was snagged in close to her, grazing her breasts.

"Here," she said, sliding his wrist down, "this will be more comfortable."

"Think so?" His eyes narrowed.

She only shook her head as he worked his hand back up her arm. His constant need to touch her was enormously seductive.

Holding her close to him, his thigh muscles brushing the skin of her bare thigh, he said, "Okay?"

She surrendered and let his arm remain, a humming electrical cord binding them.

As they sauntered over muddy ground down to the riverbanks, Sarah spotted Buck. "Hey, there, Yucky Bucky!"

A reed-thin, red-haired man with a straw cowboy hat pushed up on his head looked over. "Hey yourself, Scarey Sairy." He bent down to Nicholas, who was huddled between his legs dangling a fishpole in the murky Caloosahatchie. When Sarah called out, Nicholas gazed at them and grinned around the tag end of an ice cream cone sticking out of his mouth.

Sarah wanted to run to him and give him a rib-cracking hug, but it wasn't her right. She trailed behind Jake, who lifted Nicholas up by the seat of his britches.

"Catch anything, kid?"

"Sure, Jake, the best. Look in the bucket."

"Hi, Nicholas." Sarah allowed herself a kiss on his cheek which, bless his little-boy heart, he refrained from scrubbing off.

"Go see, Sarah. I got the best catch of the day. Buck said so."

"He did?" Sarah cocked her finger at Buck. "What have you been pulling now?"

Buck ambled over, his thumbs hooked into the skintight, faded Levi's painted on his frame. A silver buckle fastened a belt that rode low on lean hips. He nodded to Jake whom he'd met earlier when he picked up Nicholas.

"Pest," Buck said to Sarah as he leaned down and planted a smacking kiss on the top of her head. "Y'all showed up too soon. Nicholas and I had great plans for his catch." He draped an arm around her shoulders and scrutinized her. "For a skinny runt, you don't look too bad. Legs are still decent," he faked a leer. "Sorry I missed you this morning."

"I was in the shower. You should have stayed. I'd have cooked." Sarah prodded him in the ribs. "You could use some food on these bones. Haven't talked your current honey into cooking for you yet?"

"Like Atlanta, sugar, she's gone with the wind." Turning to Jake who'd joined them, Buck confided, "She ever tell you why I call her 'Scarey Sairy'?"

"No." Suddenly a stranger behind the mirrored sunglasses he'd put on, Jake glanced at her.

"Come on, Buck, don't do this," Sarah laughed and tried to pull away.

"Nope," he chivvied her, "you're not going to escape. Jake's got to hear the story."

"Can't wait." Jake's voice went so flat it was below sea level.

Sarah leaned toward him, knowing Buck's arm around her and the shared reminiscences were leaving Jake on the edge of the camp fire again. She didn't like the image of a lonely Jake prowling at the fringes of warmth and comfort, so she slipped her hand into his. "Don't believe a word Buck tells you. He wouldn't know the truth if it came wearing a name tag."

Buck pulled at the braid of hair hanging down her back. "See this hair? Well, Sarah was the littlest of the cousins, the only girl, so when she had a fever and lost all her hair, we ganged up on her. Nothing serious, but you know how mean kids can be. For months after she sprouted new hair, she was Hairy Sairy, Scarey Sairy, until one day she lit into us with a bunch of mud pies. You were something, Sarah, flinging mud pies left and right.'' Buck chortled. ''You have a temper once you cut loose.''

Sarah laughed. ''I was tired of it. Anyway, you were all bigger! Gosh, our folks were furious. At least,'' she rejoined, ''my ears didn't stick out like yours!''

''See what I mean?'' Buck appealed to Jake. ''We were spanked, but Miss Priss went for ice cream.'' He turned to Nicholas. ''Speaking of ice cream, this guy's had two double-dippers.''

''Buck! You didn't!''

''Aw, why not? This is special. Let him pig out to his little heart's content. The kid can sure put away the food. Eats as much as you did, little pig.'' He pinched her nose. ''Kid could even be yours, same kind of stubborn grit.'' He winced. ''Damn, Sarah, I'm sorry. Sometimes I forget.''

The old, familiar pain twisted inside, but she knew now that it was the reverse side of the coin and she could live with it. ''Don't worry, Buck. Everybody's walked on eggs around me for so long, it's second nature, I guess. Really,'' she insisted as he frowned, ''it's okay. I buried myself alive in Mama and Daddy's house too long, Buck.''

He hugged her tightly and whispering into her ear, teased, ''Does Tough Stuff over yonder have anything to do with it, Fairy?''

Jake didn't like the way Buck was hugging Sarah. Cousin or not, Buck was entirely too free with the hugging and kissing. Gut deep, Jake figured Buck was laying it on. He'd seen the shrewdness behind the country-boy blue eyes. With that combination, Buck would be a terror in a courtroom.

Jake didn't underestimate him. Buck, for reasons of his own, had proceeded to see which of Jake's buttons he could push. Uncomfortably, Jake admitted to himself that Buck was too successful. All of Jake's buttons were down.

Jake was relieved when Sarah changed the subject. ''What about Nicholas's prize catch?''

Looking in the bucket, Jake asked, "What do you sup
pose their plans were? This is a frog."

"Buck?"

"There's a pet parade at one, remember? Nicholas and
thought the frog had a better chance there."

Buck's guileless smile made Jake's teeth ache.

Sarah looked at Jake. "Well, I don't know. We'd nee
something to put it in."

"Kid sure likes frogs," Buck said with a bland look a
Jake.

"What do you think?" Sarah's parted lips distracte
Jake. At least she was looking at him now, and not Cousi
Good-Old-Boy-But-Watch-Your-Wallet Buck.

"Sure." Jake dropped the screen lid down. "We'll fin
something for the frog in town." He urged Sarah forward
"Let's get Nicholas."

With a forefinger, Buck dipped his hat back farther on hi
head and saluted Jake. "Be seeing y'all later, then?"

The knowing look in Buck's eyes was like a fingerna
screeching down a blackboard. Jake reined in primitive im
pulses and stomped down all kinds of territorial impera
tives. "We'll look for you."

"You do that." Buck winked at Sarah. "Bring Nichola
around any time. I like him. Sarah, will you be seeing hin
after he goes home?"

"I hope so."

Jake hated the small catch in her voice. What a mess.

"When did you say y'all were heading back?" Buc
straightened up and his sharpened gaze reminded Jake of
fox on the scent of prey. Buck would go for the jugular.

"I didn't." Jake smiled viciously just for Buck. "But I'
let you know." Jake made sure Buck saw him curve his palm
over Sarah's hip bone.

"You do that," Buck said in a level voice. "And in th
meantime, take good care of Miss Priss. We're kinda fon
of her, even though she's not much bigger than a minute.'

Jake acknowledged the warning with a nod. He knew what Buck was telling him, and if it weren't for the fact that Buck had gotten under his skin, Jake would like him. Wasn't Buck's fault Jake was on edge.

Not too many men had had the nerve to confront Jake, much less mount a frontal attack. A sneaky admiration shaped his attitude toward Buck. "I won't let anything hurt her."

Buck surveyed Jake. "Don't guess much could get past you." The underlying meaning was clear. Buck inclined his head toward Jake's arm before leaning down and kissing Sarah. "She looks to be in good hands."

"Nice talking with you, Buck." Jake wanted to leave while he could still act like a civilized man. He had to think about the emotions Buck was stirring up in him.

"Good seeing you, Scarey." Buck shoved his hands in his back pockets and, whistling, strolled towards a slim blonde surrounded by kids dangling fish on stringers.

Even though it was pleasant along the river, sweat pooled on Jake's neck. Nerve endings bristled all over his body. He wanted to run. His inner clock was ticking away like a bomb.

Sarah wandered over to Nicholas who squatted on the bank. Light dappled her legs, and shone in a nimbus around her and the boy. The mother and child looked far away and unreal to Jake, like a painting he'd seen in a museum, all muted colors and hazy contours.

Reaching them, he looked at Sarah's tender smile as she lightly touched Nicholas's hair and tweaked his ear. Such yearning and sweetness on her face. So much regret in the way she smoothed Nicholas's hair behind his ear. Jake saw everything in a painful flash.

He'd run out of time.

Chapter Eight

Jake waited for the right moment.

"When am I goin' to see real live Indians?" Squeezed between Jake and Sarah, Nicholas bounced on the truck seat.

Jake drove with his arm across the back so that he could keep the light material of Sarah's sleeve between his fingers. It was his anchor.

Now. Challenge her. Once he told her, though, he thought moodily, he'd lose Nicholas, and he couldn't bear shattering the look on her face as she watched her son. Not just yet. He couldn't tell her in front of Nicholas. There would be a better moment.

Pointing to a small girl dressed in a long, horizontally striped cotton skirt with red, black, and yellow stripes circling the material in varying widths and designs, Sarah answered Nicholas. "The Brighton Reservation is in Glades County. A lot of the kids you were fishing with are Seminoles."

"Where are their bows and arrows?" Nicholas wasn't happy. Peaceful Indians weren't his idea of adventure.

Sarah changed the subject. "Did you know the Seminoles are the only undefeated Indian tribe, Nicholas? Maybe you'll see the chief of the Seminoles at the parade."

"Well, that's something, at least," he said. "When are we going to the alligator wrestling? And the rodeo?"

Jake couldn't work up a smile when Sarah looked to him for help as she said, "I think some food first—not ice cream!—before the pet parade, right?"

"Yeah." Stopped in traffic, Jake looked out at the people passing on the sidewalk. Backed by the four pillars supporting the triangular Greek pediment of the courthouse, a small woman waved at them.

"Hey, Crystal Drake!" Sarah called out.

Royal palms, cabbage palms and live oak trees framed a picture straight out of Norman Rockwell, Jake thought, unaccountably provoked by its stability and peace. "This town looks just the way I'd imagine an old, Southern town."

"That's why I stay here. Too much of Florida has been homogenized by tourism and growth. I like a small town." Sarah split a piece of cinnamon gum three ways, handing Jake a square.

He folded it into his mouth. The flavor bit his tongue and he welcomed the sharpness because it pierced the numbness suffocating him.

It should be raining. Then he and Sarah could go home and talk. Once he'd forced the truth from her, who knows? He would kiss her and make her want him, kiss her and touch her until she understood that nothing else was important except the sweetness pouring through her. Not what she'd done, not what he'd been. Nothing was as important as what he could be with her, what she could be with him. He slapped his palm on the wheel.

"Jake?" Worry flowed under her nighttime voice.

He managed a twisted smile. "I'm hungry, too, I reckon." That was the truth of it. "Where do you want to eat?"

She chewed on her thumb. Had Nicholas picked that habit up from her? "How about hitting the food booths after we fix up Froggie here?"

"Soda?" suggested Nicholas.

"Why not?" Sarah tapped his nose. "You're already wired for sound, so how much more harm can a large dose of absolutely calorie-laden, nutritionally empty junk do you?"

"I don't know," he replied earnestly. "Let's see."

Sarah rolled her eyes at Jake. "Want me to tie a string to him so you can reel him in off the ceiling tonight when you're ready to sleep and he's not?"

"He'll crash." Jake glanced down at Nicholas who was banging on the bucket lid. "I think. If he doesn't, I'll send him in with you."

He tried not to think of Sarah in her bed.

She stretched her arms forward and up. The paler skin of her underarm lured his eyes. He wished he could follow the pale line to its disappearance down the sleeve of her blouse and farther. Of its own volition, his finger knuckled the underside of her slim arm. She shivered, and her eyelashes drifted down momentarily.

"Cold?"

She shook her head.

Jake curled two fingers over the curve of her shoulder and refused to think of where he wanted to touch her and how much.

Until he faced her with the truth he had to guard against the lure of her. He couldn't allow himself to think about touching her that way. Couldn't afford to, his damnable inner voice whined. He wanted it over.

They found a cage for the frog and gave in to Nicholas's plea that they buy a tiny dog sweater and tam-o'-shanter for F. Roggie, as Nicholas dubbed him. Jake found himself

cursing dogs and frogs as he worked the small sweater over
F. Roggie's bulbous head.

"I don't think he has the neck for sweaters," Sarah
snickered when only the frog's unblinking gaze was visible.

"No. Froggie's okay. I like him and he likes me." Nicholas eyeballed F. Roggie. "Is the sweater hurting him? He
looks like he don't like it."

Jake decided to rescue Sarah who looked as though she
needed a few seconds to steady herself. Every time she
looked at the frog, she giggled.

Before he could speak, though, she gasped, "We'll wait
and put the sweater on in time for the parade. I don't think
he likes formal clothes." She kept looking back and forth
from the frog to Jake and laughing.

"All right. What's so funny?" Surprising himself, Jake
laughed with her. He'd never had this sense of shared
laughter and companionship until Nicholas—and Sarah. It
wasn't just the physical attraction he had to resist, it was
everything about her.

"Courting," she giggled again. "Remember that old
song? 'Froggie went a-courtin'?"

"I remember." Her smile melted some of the ice encas-
ing him. "But green's not my color."

"No, indeed," she chuckled.

"If you kiss me, though, I might turn into a prince." He
intended his comment to be lighthearted, but the words
came out more seriously than he'd meant, disturbing in their
hint of something he didn't want to consider, but he liked
the way her face softened and blurred.

"That's true. You do have the soul of a prince, Jake
Donnelly." She looked at him with her blue eyes dark with
some emotion he couldn't identify.

"It's you, Sarah, you. The magic's all you," he murmured through dry lips, catching a glimpse of what might
be.

Jake raised her slight palm to his mouth and kissed the inside, softly biting the small mound of her thumb. "You, only you." He closed her fingers together, but he wanted them open and on him.

"You don't talk much, but when you do you really make your words count for something." She brushed her closed fist against his lips. "You say the loveliest things."

"You have that power over me," Jake said, following her knuckles with his mouth, knowing it was true and regretting it. "Remember that, no matter what."

"Why do you talk as though something dreadful is going to happen? You're frightening me." She stopped her fingers against his lips. "I don't want my life the way it used to be. Please, don't do this."

"Just a mood. Chalk it up to no sleep."

"I'm hungry," Nicholas interrupted.

"Well, let's go have some barbecue," Sarah said, turning to him, leaving Jake aching for something he couldn't name.

"'kay." He crawled over Sarah to the door as the truck stopped.

Dangling Nicholas with his frog cage between them, they headed into the park.

Roaming through the stalls of "chickees" decorated for the festival with replicas of bass and sawed-off palm branches, Sarah said she was hungry, too. Nicholas wanted fry bread, she wanted a cola and barbecue, and Jake snacked his way through the park from the Boy Scout troop booth to Martha Gopher's.

Jake bought swamp cabbage and teased Sarah until she was red-faced with laughter. Underneath his teasing, though, he couldn't prevent the dark current that ran strong and heavy and caused her to watch him warily.

Jake wished he had a camera when the judges handed Nicholas the trophy for Best Dressed Pet. Sarah said someone sure had a sense of humor. Nicholas said maybe they should leave the teddy bear sweater on F. Roggie. Jake said no. Sarah said no. And for the first time since he'd known him, Jake saw Nicholas throw a rip-snorting, heel-stomping, eye-popping tantrum. After everything the kid had been through and lost, he pitched a fit over a sweater on a frog. Jake was dumbfounded.

Sarah, though, pulled Nicholas onto her lap and wrapped him tightly in her arms. Carefully she removed the frog from his hands. "Stop it, Nicholas. F. Roggie isn't used to sweaters. They're not good for him. See how miserable he looks?"

"I don't care," Nicholas screamed.

"Of course you do. You're responsible for him. If you don't treat him right, he'll die." Sarah was slipping the sweater off the frog as she spoke.

Jake was responsible for Nicholas. If he did the wrong thing—

"Is that true?" Nicholas swallowed tears and rage.

"Of course it is. Truth is important. I wouldn't lie to you just to make you mind me."

"No." Nicholas accepted that.

"I hate lies." Passion roughened Sarah's words.

Her words pounded one more nail in Jake's coffin. She was so warm and loving with Nicholas. All Jake's knowledge of human nature told him he'd made a disastrous mistake. She constantly blunted the sword of his anger.

"Sometimes I lie." Nicholas's voice was small. "Do you hate me?"

"Oh, honey, of course not. I love you." She handed the frog to Jake as she said to Nicholas, "How could I hate you?" She gathered him to her. "It's hard to understand, isn't it?"

"Like teasing. I don't understand it, either." He stuck his thumb in his mouth.

"No, I suppose not." She rubbed her cheek against his hair and looked at Jake.

Her warmhearted glance swamped Jake in its wake with melancholy. Everything was slipping away from him. He cupped her elbow and rubbed the skin against her delicate bones just to reassure himself that she was there, still there. He'd wanted her in his bed even when he'd forced himself to hate her, and now when he needed to fight her sweetness and spirit, he was losing the battle. He was going to lose everything.

Sunshine wrapped them in warm amber as they sat on a bench. Tipped with gold, Sarah's eyelashes fluttered on her silky skin. Jake brushed his wrist against them, and they lifted with his touch, responding to him. The moment seeped into him, its golden peace an ointment for the sickness in his soul.

"We going to the games now?"

Squeezing Nicholas's shoulder, Jake let his fingers graze Sarah's. "Just a minute, sport." In a low voice, he checked with her and wished the moment were just what it seemed, not colored by past darkness and doubt. "Think he's too tired?"

"Probably, but we'll manage." She fluffed Nicholas's hair. "Right?"

His sniff expressed disgust. "'Course."

"No tantrums," Jake cautioned.

"I'll try." Nicholas's worried eyes searched Jake's face. "I want to go real bad. I'll be good. Okay, Jake?"

"Okay." No way in the world could he hold out against that look in the kid's eyes. If he wanted games, he could have them.

And have them he did. Nicholas strained to blow a bubble, and Jake picked gum out of his hair. Sarah lined up with him and waited for the Hay Stack Scramble. When Nicholas's turn came, he dived headfirst into the pile of hay, shrieking and laughing. He forgot to look for the candy and coins, but Sarah, caught up in the action, jumped up and down, screaming, "The candy, Nicholas! The candy!"

When Nicholas came charging out of the enclosure with candy and coins falling from his fists, Sarah whirled him in her arms as Jake watched with his booted foot angled onto the fence until Sarah and Nicholas stumbled against him, out of breath and panting.

Landing on the ground, both feet pumping, Nicholas barreled off to the sack race.

In back of Sarah, Jake steadied her with his hands on her waist. Her blouse slid and bunched under his fingers. Suppleness and silk and Sarah. He yielded to the need to touch her. He took a deep breath and nuzzled her neck, his tongue tracing a secret path under wisps of hair.

"Jake. Not here," she whispered with a shy smile.

"Why not?" he whispered back.

"People can see." But she tilted her head.

"Nobody's watching." His thumbs rested on her waist as his fingers opened and spread over her hips. "I love the feel of you," he murmured against her neck.

"Please, not here."

Her fanny brushed against him with her restless movements. He stilled her as he inhaled the scent of her skin and then stepped back from her. He'd lost. "Somewhere, Sarah. And soon."

Wiping her palms down her legs, she looked over her shoulder at him. "What about my courtship?" She cleared her throat. "I liked being courted."

He snagged the waistband of her shorts and pulled her to him. "The courtship's over."

Her eyes widened. "You make that sound like a warning."

"It is."

"I think it should be a mutual decision." Wariness edged into her eyes.

"It should be."

"Why now?"

"I can't keep on like this."

"Why the warning, then?"

"Fair play. I'm putting you on notice. The gloves are off."

She clasped her hands together. "We're not in a battle, Jake."

"Not yet." He pulled her hands apart and wedged his fingers in between hers. "But we may be."

"You're scaring me again." She rubbed her hands together.

"I mean to. I told you I'm not a good guy. Everything I said was true."

Her fingers trembled against his. "What wasn't true, Jake? Are you in trouble?" A shaky laugh accompanied her words.

"Yes." He couldn't back out now. Whatever would be, would be, but his future loomed emptily before him.

"I can help you with whatever it is," she said carefully. "Buck can solve any legal problems, believe me." At his silence, the glow in her eyes dimmed. "It's bad, isn't it?"

"Yes." He withdrew into himself, steeling himself for the next words, the words that would destroy everything. Now he knew—how could he have been such a fool as not to know before?—what he was losing. Dropping her hands, he stepped back. "I didn't plan for this." Perspiration ran down his back. "Believe me." He flipped his sunglasses over his eyes.

As he moved away, Sarah reached out to him. His eyes hidden, he'd become a stranger. All the tenderness of the last weeks disappeared as though they'd never been. His words left her shaking to the core. She didn't want to hear what he was going to say. It was going to be bad.

"You don't have to tell me anything." Pressing her knees together, she tried to stop their shaking. Don't tell me, she wanted to beg him.

Carved from stone, he stood at a distance from her, his words pounding at her. "I have to." He blocked the afternoon sun and his shadow fell over her.

"Whatever you've done, Jake, we can solve it." She swallowed. Knowing she was on safe ground, she tried to joke. "You haven't killed anybody, have you?"

His craggy face slanted to the blood-red sun. "Not lately."

"I was kidding," she said.

He turned fully to her and lifted his glasses. "I wasn't." His expression was closed off.

"You must have had a reason." If Jake had killed someone, he'd done it in self-defense. She'd talk to Buck. Buck could fix it.

Jake didn't move a muscle, but the harsh lines around his mouth eased a little. "Oh, I did."

"But—"

"You'd go bail for me, would you?" A remnant of warmth curled through his words.

"Of course." Her answer was immediate. She'd do more than that for him, if it would ease the desolation on his face. "What can I do to help you?"

At her question, he shifted his weight. "That was a long time ago, in a nasty little war. And not the problem now. I wish it was." He looked around when Nicholas tackled him at the knees. "Hello, sport."

Jake's expression as he looked at Nicholas frightened Sarah.

"I was last in the sack race." Nicholas said. "Me and my partner kept falling down. On purpose. It was the greatest."

"Good for you." Jake threw Nicholas up in the air and caught him, swinging him again and again before settling him on his shoulders. Holding Nicholas's fists in his, Jake spoke to Sarah. "Later."

Her breath flew out of her lungs as if she'd been thumped in the stomach. Something loomed on the horizon that threatened to shatter the life she'd begun rebuilding. Everything that had started with Jake knocking on her door was coming to a head.

This time, though, she was going to be in charge. Never again would she be a victim. No one was going to yank the reins of choice out of her control this time. Whatever Jake told her, she'd handle. Whatever she had to do, she'd do.

Sarah let Nicholas run interference. She needed time to sort out her emotions and thoughts. Avoiding Jake, she concentrated on Nicholas and tried to ignore the fear nibbling away at her, tried to ignore, too, the stab of Jake's glance every time she moved. Once, looking up from tying Nicholas's sneaker, she surprised Jake as he watched her. Desire, possessiveness and despair swam in the brown depths of his eyes as they trailed along the length of her bent legs.

The red sun burned into twilight. There would be a storm.

At a little before eleven that night, they hit the midway for Chalo Nitka Midnight Madness.

Sarah didn't like midways, but she'd promised Nicholas. In the flashing lights and nightmare world of the carny, faces were distorted, the familiar turned inside out by garish greens and reds.

A whipping wind tossed pennants and banners and stung her eyes with drops of rain. The sky glowed with reflected oranges and its own storm colors against fast-moving dark clouds blowing in from the east.

Overwhelmed by the strangeness of the sights and sounds, Nicholas rode Jake's shoulders and grew quiet. Darting, shrieking figures dodged in and out, bumping against the booths and people. Sarah noticed that no one bumped into the three of them. Jake's rock-like solidity and the expression on his face discouraged contact.

"Hey, Priss, having a good time?" Buck emerged from the shadows near the Ferris wheel.

At the sudden movement, Jake's shoulders rolled and tightened as he gripped Nicholas's ankles and stepped in front of Sarah.

"Whoa, big guy. Just ole Buck here." He ambled up to them. "How's the fisherman?" He reached up and gave Nicholas a high five. Perched on top of Jake, Nicholas returned a low three. "I came to see if Little Stuff here wanted to keep me company on some of the rides." Buck checked Jake's face for permission before cocking his head at Nicholas. "Think you're up to it?"

"'kay."

"Well, time's a'wastin'. Let's hit the stomach-scramblers and see." Buck grabbed Nicholas's hand and strolled off to the tilt-a-whirl.

As they disappeared into the lights and noise, Sarah regretted the loss of Nicholas's protection. She knew the next few moments were going to change her life.

Gripping her elbow hard, Jake piloted her towards a small section in back of the merry-go-round. "We have to talk. I can't take any more." Electrical cables snaked around their feet, but he led her through the maze to a clear spot lit by the circling lights of the carousel as it wheeled round and round. "Sit down."

With his rigid face and flat, mechanical voice, he was a robot, not the man she'd known these last weeks, not—and the knowledge burst upon her like fireworks—not the man she'd been falling in love with as slowly and inexorably as tides moving to the pull of the moon.

"I lied to you, Sarah, right from the beginning."

Harsh, ugly, the words fell on her ears like a cracked bell tolling. Fear immobilized her. It had been five years since terror had seized her so absolutely. She remembered it and the helplessness it brought.

Childlike, she pressed her hands over her ears, cutting off the words crashing over her. Jake's soundless lips moved.

Then, in an iron grip, he forced her hands down. "I didn't show up at your door by accident. But you knew that."

"Yes."

"You just never figured out why."

Unbearable suspicions were raising their snaky heads in her mind, suspicions she'd ignored over and over because they were too crazy. Somewhere inside she reached for courage and found it. "Go on."

"I'd been driving around for hours trying to decide whether I ought to give you a chance. I kept thinking I had to see you for myself." His fingers bit into her wrists.

"Why should you think you owed me a chance? A chance at what, Jake?"

In the background, Sarah heard soft laughter from the children on the merry-go-round. Red and green and yellow, its lights flashed on Jake's hard features. His mouth slashed white in the green when he spoke.

"I hated you." He shook his head. "And then you came to the door and everything went right out of my head, everything Ted had told me, everything I believed about you."

"You knew my husband? And you never told me?" It was going to be worse than she'd even imagined. She closed her hands around his imprisoning fingers until her nails sank into his skin.

"I knew Ted. I'd known him earlier, and then I ran into him again on a job in the Middle East. He had his son with him."

Sarah moaned. "When?" She was swallowing dry heaves.

"Last year."

"You're lying! That's not possible!" she said. "They died four years ago."

Jake stood, dragging her to her feet. "They didn't. Ted looked me up early this year. He was dying. He said he'd pay me to take his son back to America, but there was one condition.''

"What are you saying?'' She grabbed his shirt and shook him. "What are you telling me?'' She knew, *she knew*, but it wasn't possible. She'd convinced herself of that impossibility over and over again.

Fierce, like a hawk ripping at its prey, he spoke. "I'm saying Ted paid me to bring his son back to America on the condition that I never let the boy's mother know he was alive.'' Gripping her shoulders in his powerful hands, he pulled her to him. "I'm telling you I brought Ted's son to America.''

She struggled against him, rage engulfing her. He was plunging her into a nightmare.

"And I told myself I had to see if his mother was fit to raise the son she'd abandoned, just as I'd been abandoned. I owed her that.''

Sarah's slap against his hard features was soundless in the carnival noise, but she heard his words.

"And I found you.''

Her question forced itself past clenched teeth. "Nicholas?'' Tears streamed from her eyes. "You bastard! Nicholas is my son, isn't he, isn't he?''

"Ted's son. The one you left behind when you fled to safety, Sarah. Your son.''

Chapter Nine

Sarah couldn't think, couldn't breathe. Everything shut down on her. She bit her lip and didn't feel pain. The cold-eyed, blank-faced stranger in front of her was proving to her that reality didn't exist. Idiot-like, she parroted, "My son?"

"Your son," he affirmed. "Ted's, yours. Nicholas." He folded his arms across his chest and stood there, his empty eyes watching her.

Her knees buckled and she looked around, wondering how she found herself on the hard-packed dirt. Jake sank next to her and reached out a hand.

"Don't—don't touch me. Don't you dare," she spat, anger once more bringing sensations with it—the damp of the earth, the rawness of her lip where she'd bitten it, the tinny waltz of the carousel. Blindly, she flicked his hand away like a loathsome insect and tried to scramble to her feet. "Nicholas. Where is he? I want him!"

In a frenzy, Sarah scrutinized the crowds. She had to get to Nicholas.

"Sit down." Jake's voice was rough, and his hand clamped around her arm. "You're not going anywhere until you've heard me out. We're settling this."

If she didn't know better, she'd think she heard pain in his voice. "Explain? What can you possibly say to explain this? And how could I believe anything you said?" Bitterness spurted out. "You've lied to me from the first moment. Who's to say you're not lying now?"

"I'm not lying." Anger blazed from him.

"So you say." She pulled against his hand. "Turn me loose."

"Not until you listen to me."

"What if I don't?" she said.

"Then you'll never know the truth." He sighed but didn't free her. "Listen, Sarah. Please. I can't go on like this. It's killing me."

It was the sorrow in his voice that swayed her, a sorrow that rang true. "All right. Tell me." Knowing he wouldn't let her go to Nicholas, she sagged to the ground.

"I've messed this up from the beginning." From far away his words sank into her. "But there's been enough deception."

"I'm not arguing." Drained, she looked at Jake's face, the face of a man she'd been on the verge of loving—maybe already did—the face of a stranger now in the tawdry midway lights. "Go ahead. What is the *truth*?"

Jake hunkered over her. "I knew Ted before he married you. We met while I was consulting on a job. He'd been hired to teach the American workers about the language and politics of the country. He was a well-known expert, and the oil company hoped it could short-circuit potential problems if he briefed us on hot issues."

"Oh, yes," Sarah said as grief seeped into her, "Ted was the expert, all right. He cared for that country more than he did anything else, certainly more than he loved me or my baby."

"He was there to convince the workers that they had to look at things from the eastern viewpoint, not to insist on their American ways of doing things. He made sure they knew what would be considered insulting." Jake bent closer and his heat and anger enveloped her. "We became friends of a sort. He was easy to like."

Sarah covered her eyes for a moment, remembering the man who'd charmed her into marriage and talked her into going back with him to the country he'd adopted, remembered him, too, as the father of her child. "Ted spent most days and nights at the university. He became a fanatic about the Middle East and its problems. A convert. He didn't want to come back home."

Her voice trickled away as her memories crowded in. She'd tried to obliterate the past in order to survive in the present, and now Jake was bringing it all back.

Jake pulled her hands away from her eyes. "Look at me when I talk to you, Sarah. I want to see your face. I want you to look into my eyes and then dare accuse me of lying." Ruthless and determined, he stripped her of her defenses.

"You're heartless."

"I told you the gloves were off, but you're going to hear me out and you're going to face me when you do. No more walls. No more hiding. For either of us."

Sarah knew he was right even though she hated him. He'd kept her son from her. "I'm listening." She'd endure what she had to and then go on. She could do that now.

Jake gripped her arm tighter. "When Ted ran into me, I could tell he was desperate. He looked as though he'd been living hand-to-mouth. He knew he was dying and begged me to take the boy to America."

"I don't understand. The State Department told me they'd been killed in a bombing." All this time her son had been alive and she'd given up because some blue suit had told her he was dead. She should have known better. Sarah

ubbed her knees, the repetitive motion calming in the midst
of the turmoil. "What happened?"

Jake shrugged. "I don't know. I figured out that he'd
been in hiding, but I couldn't get him to tell me what was
going on. You know how unsettled politics are over there."

"To my everlasting grief, I do." Sarah clenched her fists.

"Anyway, I didn't pry."

"How admirable. You were stupid not to." She shook her
head.

Jake frowned. "Yes." He straightened her fingers, one by
one. "But I was back in that country with my own job to do.
I was supposed to slip an oil executive threatened with kid-
napping out of the country before anyone missed him. His
company hired me to go in undercover, so when I ran into
Ted I couldn't ask too many questions. I couldn't afford to
answer any of my own."

"But how could you not ask some questions?" Jake's
attitude was beyond her.

"Look," Jake's irritation reached her, "I didn't ask
questions because I didn't want to explain myself and,
frankly, I didn't give a damn what was going on with Ted. I
looked at his kid and made up my mind. No kid should have
been carted around like that. I'd have done anything then to
get the boy out of that country. It wasn't safe for him." Jake
slammed his hands under his armpits. "But I don't suppose you'd understand that."

"Of course not. I was only his mother." Coming from her
tight throat, her sarcastic words were rusty. "Why did you
agree to Ted's conditions?"

"It was the only way I could get the kid from him," Jake
snarled. "What was I supposed to do? At that point, I'd
have told Ted anything. Besides," Jake's voice grew men-
acing, "Ted told me all about the kid's mother. About how
she'd deserted both of them, running back to America because she couldn't stand life in the Middle East, told me how
he begged her to stay with the baby—"

"What?" Sarah leaped to her feet.

Jake rose, towering above her, anger and threat rolling over her. "How he *begged* her not to abandon their son, how she laughed in his face while she packed her bags. Any of this sound familiar, Sarah Jane Simpson? Or should I say Sarah Jane Harrison? That was your married name, wasn't it?"

The savage edge to Jake's voice should have intimidated her, and once it would have, but not anymore—not with the miracle of her son in range of her breath and voice. "None of what you're saying is true. It never happened." Cold and in control now, she continued, "I don't know how Ted managed to sell you such a story, but you were played for a sucker."

"Really?" He said in a voice soft with warning. "Now just how could that be? Remember? I was there in the dust and rubble. And you were here in your home, safe and warm." Jake curled his hands over her shoulders. "Did you ever think about the son you left behind, Sarah? About his being cold or hungry?" His fingers tightened. "Because when I found him, he was both."

His words battered her and she swayed. "Don't! I can't bear to hear it. I never stopped thinking about him." She wiped away the streaming tears. "Never."

"How touching." Jake pushed her away. "I could almost believe you, but I was there. I saw Ted. He loved his son. His wife's desertion broke him."

Sarah wiped the tears from her face. She'd been in pain before, but ignorance had blunted it. Knowing what her son had gone through was worse than imagining, and she'd imagined everything, everything, but knowing was worse and she attacked. "You took the money. You agreed to Ted's condition. That doesn't say much for your nobility."

"I turned the money down." Jake wiped his hands down his jeans. "But I agreed not to let the boy's mother know about him. Ted had reason to ask that."

"How could you agree to such a monstrous proposal?" She couldn't afford to lose control.

"After what she'd done, she didn't deserve Nicholas." Flat and judgmental, Jake's statement left no room for the grays of human behavior.

"I see." Brushing her eyes again, Sarah found the courage to continue. "What if you were wrong?"

"When I met you, I thought I was, but you never explained things, not even when I gave you the chance."

"I didn't think my past was any of your business." Sarah faced him down. "But you decided to force yourself into my life and play God."

"Yes."

"Why?"

Jake paced away from her. "I didn't know what to do about Nicholas. I'm a loner. I couldn't give him what he needed, a home, stability, settledness—all those small-town virtues," Jake snarled. "I couldn't give him those things, and I wasn't going to dump him on some child-welfare department. I know what that's like, so I thought, what the hell, I'd see his mother for myself. Maybe he'd be better off with me. I had to know."

"And you stayed." Memories, hot and treacherous, swirled between them with her words.

"Yes."

"Trying to decide whether or not I was *fit* to have my own son?" Sarah grabbed his shirt and made him look at her. "Didn't the weight of playing God ever get to you, Jake? Even God rested, so I've been told, but you just stayed on and on pretending to court me, judging me."

"It wasn't like that."

"Of course it was. Lies and deception and you playing God. That's just what it was. All lies, all pretending."

"No, not everything. I—" He touched her hair gently.

"You what, Jake? Decided that maybe I'd been in the grip of some postpartum depression? Made excuses for me?'' Sarah lost it. Anger and hurt and fury boiled out of her. ''Or just decided that I was worthless?''

''I wanted you.''

His somber words stopped her. ''Want? How could you want a woman you thought had abandoned her son? Especially since your mother had deserted you?''

''I don't know.'' His face looked as though it had been scoured clean of all emotion. ''But I did.''

''Am I supposed to fall in your arms now that you've explained everything? Is that what you expect?''

His face was grim. ''I don't expect anything.''

''Does that excuse what you did to me?'' Sarah wanted to howl with anguish. He'd destroyed whatever they could have had together. She'd been building dreams on shifting sand, and the tide was crashing in, washing them out to sea. She'd been stupid. Now she had to salvage what she could for herself.

Jake heard her words and knew he'd blown it. ''I don't have an excuse. I found myself in a situation I didn't choose. I did the best I could.''

''What about honesty? Why didn't you try that?''

Her pale face and suffering eyes wrenched him, but stubbornly he pushed ahead. He had to make her see how it was. ''I couldn't. Nicholas's life was at stake. Can't you understand how I felt? How could I leave him with someone who'd already dumped him?''

''But after? When you knew I wasn't like that? Or didn't you ever reach that conclusion?'' Rain drops and tears wet her eyelashes.

Jake exhaled. ''I couldn't leave him. I couldn't leave you.''

When he looked into her eyes, he drowned in her pain and knew the rack was being tightened one more notch.

''Do you know what you did to me?'' Her hands were moving in agitation. ''Do you want to know what really happened five years ago?''

"If you want to tell me." Jake didn't know what else to say. Her pale face worried him. The anger that had bubbled up when he was recalling Ted's story and confronting her with it had vanished in the misty rain. Looking at her, he knew without a doubt that Ted had lied. Had known it since he'd first seen her, but he'd refused to admit it.

Like the ripple of water betraying the passage of deep-swimming fish, memory shivered over her face.

"I was young, twenty-one, just finishing college when I met Ted. He was handsome, brilliant, and I worshipped him. He was from an old Charleston family and swept me off my feet. He was the golden man of every girl's dreams."

Jake hated Ted.

She continued pensively. "I thought it was romantic that he wanted me to follow him back to the Middle East where he was on a professorship, and it was. Until my son was born."

She never referred to the boy as *their* son, just *hers*.

"Then Ted changed. He resented any time I spent with the baby. Of course it was all right that he was never home, always in meetings with people he never introduced me to. When I learned some of them were involved in a coup against the government, I was terrified." Sarah's voice shook.

"What did you do?" Jake could see it all now. What a fool he'd been.

"What any mother would do. I tried to talk Ted into leaving. I tried—oh, God in heaven, how I tried—to make him see how his political maneuverings were putting us in danger."

Jake watched the raindrop—a tear?—slide down her face. "Why didn't you take your son and leave?"

Sarah's laugh grated against him. "That does seem simple, doesn't it? I tried, but when I told Ted the baby and I were going home, he went berserk."

His Sarah, Sarah, who would never be his, scraped her hands against her jeans over and over. Jake wanted to capture them and calm their fluttering distress.

Her husky voice, tear-washed and thin, slashed into him. "Do you know what that meant? From that moment on, I was never alone. The nurse Tardeh, Ted, one of his friends' wives, someone was always around. Don't you see, Jake?" she said quietly. "Ted had no intention of letting us go without him, and he wouldn't leave. Not even when our embassy was bombed. That was when I knew I had to get us out."

Jake leaned against a booth and folded his arms as he thought through the possibilities, knowing from experience how difficult it would have been. "What did you do?"

Low and muffled by the storm of carnival noise, her voice still flowed into every pore of his body. In the damp air, her flower scent taunted him with memories.

"I begged him to go with us, I promised him I'd return with him if we could at least take the baby home to America."

Jake closed his hands over her chilled palms. She never noticed, and her cold fingers continued their agitated fluttering. He dropped his hands. He couldn't even give her comfort.

"Finally he agreed."

"So what happened?" Jake remembered Ted, his facile charm. With heaviness in his heart, Jake now knew what Ted had done.

"Ted bought the tickets, made the plans, helped me pack." Sarah's voice was cracking and Jake stepped closer. "We boarded the plane." She laughed wildly. "It would be the last plane out of there, but none of us on it knew that at the time."

Jake was afraid to touch her. The undertow of memory sucked her away from him, far away to a distant shore and time.

"We were buckled in our seats. Already buckled in! Can you imagine? So close. And then Ted looked out the window. 'There's Tardeh,' he said."

The clutch of her small, cold fingers chilled Jake bone-deep. So much wrong had been done.

"'Let me take the baby down to see her for a moment. It's the last time she'll ever see him, Sarah. Don't turn against Tardeh, too. She's been his second mother.'" Sarah shook her head and the damp braid slithered against Jake's arm. "I protested a little. I told Ted the baby needed his bottle, that he was tired."

Sarah looked right through Jake. "Ted stood up. I remember he bumped his head." Her face twisted in reminiscence. "I told him to hurry, I wanted to give the baby his bottle as he took off so his ears—" She paused and her mouth quivered. "So his ears wouldn't hurt." Frantically she pulled her hands free and rubbed her arms. "Is it getting colder?" she said plaintively.

"Not really. Stand over here. I'll block the wind." Jake faced the spitting wind. They were going to have to leave before the skies opened. Buck and Nicholas would be coming back any minute. He glanced up. A few heavy clouds with a front moving in.

Still she rubbed her arms. "I kept watching for Ted to come down the aisle." She looked down at the ground. "I'll never forgive myself for that. How could I have risked my child by trusting Ted?" Blindly she looked up at Jake.

"Ted's child, too, Sarah," Jake emphasized.

Over and over she rubbed her hands. "He was so hungry and kept sucking my thumb—" Her sob was dry and old. "I was so careless. Ted kept at me and at me and I let him take my baby."

"It wasn't your fault."

Her look was uncomprehending. She was in another world and time.

"I touched his sleepy little eyelids—so droopy and silky. I still feel them at night in my dreams, that baby-silk against my fingers. Oh God, I still wake up thinking I'm on the plane holding him and Ted is reaching for him and I hold my baby tighter and tighter and don't let go and the plane takes off with him still in my arms, still wrapped in his blue blanket with white puffs, and I reach down to smooth his silky skin—''

"Sweetheart, don't," Jake reached out for her. Her pain was destroying him.

"Robbie," she murmured, rubbing her empty hands together and looking around at a world gone insane with Ferris wheels and merry-go-rounds.

"Nicholas," corrected Jake. "Ted changed his name after you left. God only knows why. If he wanted to make finding them more difficult, he should have changed both of their names. He didn't, though, and the kid only knows himself as Nicholas. You can't confuse him now by calling him Robbie."

He was just understanding the enormity of what he'd done to this woman with her fragile face and courageous heart. He'd kept her son from her. She'd never forgive or forget that.

Like a winter wind, the loneliness of life without Sarah blew through Jake, freezing the tender shoots sprouting in his soul. He tasted salty rain in the air and realized it was his own tears. He couldn't remember ever shedding tears before. Once again he covered her empty, seeking hands with his.

He wanted to kill Ted for causing Sarah such pain. Bitterly Jake realized how he'd been taken in. Ted had known Jake's past and used it against him, against Sarah. "Ted planned it?"

"It would never have worked if I hadn't been so gullible. I should have known better, but I believed him. I have no one to blame but myself, my own stupidity."

Jake knew Sarah would have fought like a woman possessed for her son. Why had he resisted that knowledge for so long and used his anger to twist his feelings about Sarah into hostility? The answer seeped into his heart. Nicholas. He'd grown to think of Nicholas as his own and couldn't give him up.

"What did you do after you got home?" Jake sought refuge in speech from his disturbing thoughts. She shrugged. "I don't remember very clearly. There was a doctor on the plane who gave me a sedative, and from that point on I blanked everything out for months. I made hundreds of phone calls and used every contact I could to reach anyone who could help me. I even put an ad in a mercenaries' magazine. Buck says he told me not to, but that I screamed and yelled at him and did it anyway."

Jake wanted to wrap her in his arms and never let anyone, including himself, hurt his Sarah again. But he'd messed up the chance to do that. Soft as drifting spume, her voice interrupted his thoughts. "Then I was told they'd been killed in a terrorist bombing, and the world turned gray. Until now." Her glance accused him.

Even after promising not to, he'd hurt her. Defensively, Jake jammed his hands in his back pockets. He'd hurt her, but he'd also brought Nicholas to her. Ted had taken her son, not him. He wasn't Ted.

Desperation urged him into action. He'd always been more comfortable going on the offensive. "I did what I thought was right." She had to accept that.

"You still don't get it, do you, Jake?" Sarah looked at him, her eyes drowned in tears.

He wouldn't let her shove him out of her life this easily. A barely comprehended hurt pushed him. Slouching on one hip, he drawled, "I understand I brought your son back to you." Fear generated anger and overrode caution. "And I understand that I can have you any time I want you." He yanked her to him, holding her against his hard, rain-damp length.

Sad and mournful, like slivers of glass on terrazzo, her words pierced him as nothing else ever had. "Once. Not any more. You want, you take. That's not what I need in my life, Jake. I need love."

"So help me learn." He'd use whatever weapon he could. He opened his mouth over hers in a claiming he'd not known he was capable of. Again and again he sought the sweetness of her mouth which lay cool and unresponsive under his. Shoving her against the damp boards of the booth he touched her, smoothed her hair sparkling with carousel lights and mist, and murmured dark words of passion and love he'd never said before, moved his seeking fingers over her. Nothing he did changed her marble-cool lips to the soft warmth of Sarah. Nothing.

One last time he let himself surge into the honey of her mouth, tasted her, sought the deepest recesses of her mouth with his stroking, hungry tongue. Heaven. Hell.

"Love is more than this, Jake." Sarah stepped back, not even bothering to wipe away his kisses. "If you loved me, you'd have told me about Nicholas. You couldn't have waited this long. Every time I came close to the truth, you lied to me. Is that your definition of love, Jake? Because it's not mine." Sarah looked around her before brushing off her jeans.

"Maybe I don't know love as you define it, Miss Simpson." Deliberately, Jake insulted her. "My definition leans more to passionate kisses and long, slow nights in bed." He was furious with frustration and pain. How could she dismiss the way she felt in his arms? He had to find a way to convince her that what he'd done wasn't as black-and-white as she was making it.

"Well, you should have no trouble falling in love again, then," she said. "Try any street corner. In the meantime, I want to get Nicholas and go home."

Jake flexed his fingers. He wanted to rip the booth behind him apart, board by board. "What does that mean, precisely?"

Slowly and precisely, she told him. "It means Nicholas and I are going to the house with Buck. You can go where you want to. But I want you gone."

"And what are you going to tell Nicholas when I don't show up?"

"I'll start with the truth," she said, her clear gaze searching the shadows around her.

Jake spoke through clenched teeth. "Won't work. You'll have a hysterical kid on your hands. Anyway, do you think it's fair to uproot him again? You've been talking about love. Explain, if you can, please, how that fits into your definition." He couldn't help lashing out like a wounded animal with its paw caught in a trap gnawing at itself in pain.

"All right. You can tell him. Then you leave." The soft contours of her face tightened with determination.

"You have it all worked out, don't you?" Acid dripped from his voice. "And how do you propose to make me?"

"What?" She frowned.

"What if I decide I don't want to leave?"

"Why would you want to stay?" Bewilderment was in her voice.

He hadn't come this far to lose the only thing that had ever given shape and meaning to his life. "I love you. I love Nicholas. I've never loved anyone the way I love both of you." Rough and primitive, the feelings poured out. "I found something with you I didn't know existed."

He hadn't even known he loved her until the words came out from some deep well inside. When had it happened? And how? Maybe when he first saw her, or that day in the boat, but there was no way out for him now. The words were all said.

A flicker of compassion moved over her face, and he seized on it.

"What I did, I did at first because I loved Nicholas. Is that so wrong?" He rolled his shoulders in frustration.

"Poor Jake." She sighed. "You really don't know about love and trust, do you?" She raked her hair back. "I loved and trusted one man and it cost me my child." At last her hands stilled. "And I was falling in love with you."

She held up a hand to stop him as he began to speak. "I was bewitched by the way I felt with you and the way you acted with Nicholas. And once more I trusted where I shouldn't have. You'd have taken my son away, too."

A cow horn's raucous blast split the air.

"You must have been satisfied every time I kissed you back." Her lip trembled and Jake touched the corner.

"Never. I only wanted more. Everything you could give." He realized that was true, and he wasn't going to give up now, now when he could see what life might be like.

"Anyway, Jake, it's not important. I want you gone. I don't think I could look at you day after day and remember what almost was."

"I'm not going, Sarah." Jake stepped back, giving her all the room in the world. Not important? How could she dismiss everything he felt so casually? "I'm not going until I'm ready to. And I'm not ready."

"You don't have any say-so." Her face empty of anger, passion, love, empty of everything except a distant sadness, she shrugged as she said, "I'll have Buck draw up whatever legal papers it takes to keep you away."

Jake didn't think she could be that merciless, but just the thought of being kept away from her and Nicholas crucified him. "You do that, Sarah," he said, knowing he was digging his own grave but not knowing what else to do, "and I'll be out of here with Nicholas so fast it'll make your head swim." He gripped her tightly.

"You wouldn't!"

"Sweetheart, I'm the guy that sneaked the kid out on fake papers. If you go to Buck, you'll never see Nicholas again. I can hide anywhere I want to. I'm the kind of guy you can't trust, remember?" Acid ate at his stomach.

"I don't think you could do that to me or to Nicholas."

"Maybe not." He hooked his thumbs onto his pockets. "But are you willing to bet on it?"

Chapter Ten

Riding home in the truck down the dark, rain-slick highway, Sarah held Nicholas in her lap while rage and confusion battled in her. She couldn't stop touching him and regretting all the lost years. She brushed his funny little ears and recognized now they were just like Buck's at that age. No wonder she'd kept thinking about her lost son. Every time she'd looked at Nicholas, he'd stirred her subconscious. No wonder she'd thought she was losing her mind. But now he was in her arms, for real, not just in dreams.

An unapproachable Jake drove carefully, his thoughts hidden. Tiny snores bubbled up from Nicholas, and Sarah leaned against the door so that he could stretch out.

At the midway Buck had returned with Nicholas, registered the tension and left at Sarah's urging. His dark red eyebrows lifted in question. At the shake of her head, he'd shrugged and mouthed, "Call me."

An intimidating presence, Jake said nothing, merely stared at Buck with narrowed eyes in an otherwise expressionless face. He didn't keep her from talking with Buck, but Sarah wasn't ready to challenge Jake and risk his disappearing with Nicholas.

Now, the miles sliding by, Sarah pictured herself tied on an old-time cartoon bomb with its lit fuse fizzing closer and closer.

With her son held close to her, though, she was determined to control events. Into a silence thick with submerged emotions, she finally spoke. "I don't want Nicholas to know about all this tonight. He's too tired. Let me know before you tell him anything."

Jake slanted a look at her. "Fair enough."

"And don't go off alone with him." Her voice wavered despite her best efforts. The thought of once again losing him was unbearable.

The truck sped up before dropping back to the speed limit. Jake's expression never changed.

"I mean it, Jake." Anger clipped her words.

"You planning to stay up all night, every night, Sarah? Or bell me like a cat so you'll know any time I move?" His fingers curled tightly around the wheel. "Lots of luck, sweetheart. If I decided to disappear, believe me, I wouldn't leave a trace. That's the advantage of having no ties or roots."

"Jake," she gasped, turning to him.

At her strangled sound, he continued. "Of course, you might try to get in touch with the companies I've consulted for, but since I've only worked for them on an as-needed basis, you won't get much information." His lips tightened. "So you'd be up a creek without the proverbial paddle if you push me." Headlights from an approaching car splashed across his taut face. Darkness again as he continued. "Don't push me, Sarah."

"In other words, not one living soul on this planet would miss you if you disappeared in a puff of smoke?" She believed him. She knew his history.

"That's about it." Slapping the turn signal on, he punctuated his words with its clickety-clicking. "I told you the gloves were off, sweetheart."

"So you did." Sarah heard his harsh breathing and turned away. "Don't go off alone, Jake. I won't tell you again." The lines were drawn.

Sarah carried in "F. Roggie" while Jake carted Nicholas upstairs. She wanted to insist that Nicholas sleep with her, but one look at Jake's tightly controlled face stifled the words.

Nicholas squalled. Jake was patient. Nicholas yelled. Jake turned him upside down and wheelbarrow-walked him to the bathroom. Moving fast, Jake peeled off Nicholas's muddy jeans while Nicholas giggled. The two of them disappeared into the cloud of steam boiling out of the bathroom.

Sarah heard splashing sounds, towels flapping, Nicholas sighing. When he came out, flushed and half asleep, he clung to a towel-wrapped Jake.

The pink-and-white striped bath towel should have looked ridiculous slung around Jake's lean hips. It didn't. The small boy cradled in his arms should have looked out of place. Yet nothing had ever looked so right. Jake's chest was made for cuddling small boys—and big girls—Sarah thought. Dark hair angled to the frivolous towel knotted at his navel.

Had things been different she might have strolled boldly up to him, winked, slid her finger to the knot and tested its reliability. The dull throb of longing would die, though, soon enough.

"Sorry, this was all I could find."

"No problem," Sarah said through a constricted throat. The muscles under Jake's ribs twisted with his movement and Sarah resented him for still being able to make her ache for him.

"I want Sarah to tell me a story," Nicholas yawned. "In her room."

"Come on, sport, let's just go to bed. I'll tell you a story, okay?" Jake strode to the bedroom, his calves flexing and sleeking down to the high arch of his feet.

Beautiful feet, Sarah thought, like his hands. Dressed, Jake was all bulk. Stripped, his body showed smooth, coiling strength and muscle, perfectly shaped and proportioned.

"Want Sarah."

At Nicholas's words, Jake's eyes burned on her. Her skin flushed with the heat flaring through her.

"Whatever you want, sport." Jake settled Nicholas under the sheets in her room, and, turning to go, spoke. "Sarah—"

"Not now."

He inhaled. "You sure?"

"Yes. Not tonight. Whatever it is will wait until tomorrow. We'll deal with it tomorrow. Go to bed, Jake."

Tension reached out to her from him, from his broad, bare chest, from the ridged planes of his face. For a moment she wondered if she could make him leave, if his determination would bend in the face of her insistence.

"Your decision," he finally said, sliding his palm down over the light switch and leaving them in the muted light from the hall.

Sarah felt the slow glide of his palm as though it were moving over her throat. She swallowed. She hadn't expected this—this *wanting*—to survive after what he'd done to her.

"G'night, Jake."

"Sleep tight, sport."

Jake's wide back blocked the light and Sarah saw his shoulders slump before straightening. He left the door partially open behind him and his feet thudded softly on the carpet.

The smell of Nicholas, warm and soapy, rose to Sarah in the silence. Cuddled next to her, he watched her with sleepy blue eyes. Her eyes. "Tell me a story about when you were a kid."

"Well, a long, long time ago, in a faraway place—"

"Like space?"

"A more magical place where a small blue-eyed boy—"

"Like me?"

"Just like you, honey, just the same."

Nicholas's eyes drifted shut. Lightly, lightly, Sarah touched his eyelids. Silky still.

She'd been cheated of so much.

Sometime in the night, the frantic beating of her heart woke her and she looked up to see Jake leaning against the doorway. Nicholas slept against her, a small lump at her side.

Silence stretched between them, a living river flowing and touching, a current of longing and frustration.

"What do you want?" she whispered.

Like a wave, Jake's yearning undulated against her. Motionless, his shadow answered her. "You."

"I know." She wondered if he could hear her heart pounding.

"It's not over, Sarah."

"Go to bed, Jake."

His shadow moved soundlessly down the hall, and Sarah heard the click of his bedroom door.

Sarah stared out the window into endless night. What was she going to do? How were they going to survive in a siege state? Eventually she drifted asleep, waking with each creaking sound, her heart banging against her ribs.

For the next four days, rain squalls blew in and out. In the afternoons a watery sun shone weakly through gray skies. Sarah and Jake maintained a polite distance, walking warily through the mine fields all around them. Sarah cancelled her fishing clients and stayed near Nicholas and Jake. She held on to her anger, nursing it, feeding it, hating the way she felt around Jake.

Habit eased them through the days although Sarah took to slamming cabinet doors and banging pots and pans. She shoved all the towels off the bathroom shelves, emptied the kitchen cabinets, poured a bottle of Lysol in a bucket and worked until she was so tired she could drop. She couldn't sleep.

She yanked off the dining-room wallpaper, making Nicholas roar with laughter as flakes of powdery glue and backing showered them. Nicholas lifted the long strips up and trailed them around over his head, billowed them across the dining table, and crowed that this was neat stuff.

Sarah couldn't eat.

Nights she wandered down to the kitchen and heated milk. All she had to show for her effort was scorched pans. She didn't know what she wanted.

She couldn't understand Jake. What had made him think he had the right to play with all their lives the way he had? Why couldn't he see what a terrible thing he'd set in motion?

The questions drove her from bed to the kitchen and back, and still she couldn't sleep or forgive.

Jake watched her all the time just as she watched him. Nothing showed on his blank face. She knew when he was around, no matter how quietly he approached. No need to bell him, not with her nerve endings alive to his presence.

She and Nicholas were building a leaf boat to float in the puddles that lined the driveway, and Jake was taking advantage of the sunshine to paint the porch. He'd crashed a can of white paint down on the kitchen table that morning and hadn't said anything. The swish of his brush against the old wood counterpointed Nicholas's chatter.

Picking up another small leaf, she jabbed the twig through it, anchoring it to the larger bottom leaf. "Here, Nicholas. See if it floats, okay?" She touched the tender column at the back of his neck. So fragile.

Hurling himself off the top step, he collapsed in a heap. He sprang up and then ran in long, swerving loops down the driveway to the biggest puddle. Sarah smiled.

Leaning back against the stoop, she surprised Jake with his mask down. The paint brush stilled as he met her eyes, and small white drops plopped onto the floor.

The loneliness that had always pulled at her was a naked hunger. Once again he was the wolf prowling on the outskirts, and her heart softened fleetingly before she looked down at the crushed leaf in her hand. She brushed her hands clean and cleared her throat. Maybe she'd go sail boats with Nicholas.

She never thought of him as Robbie. Robbie was the baby who haunted her dreams. The Nicholas whose energy propelled him and her through the awkward days was the child of her heart and present. Her child would always be Nicholas to her now, never again Robbie. She stood up. The wooden steps creaked.

Jake tapped the rim of the can with his brush. "Sarah, I'm going to tell Nicholas today. Do you want to be there?" The bristles shh-shhed on the can as he worked out excess paint.

Did she? Which would be easier for Nicholas? "Let me think about it." She rubbed the sole of her sneakers against the edge of the step. "Tell me something, will you, Jake?"

"All right." His smooth strokes spread gleaming white paint over the faded boards he'd already scraped.

Needing to see his reaction, she faced him. "If you could do it all over, would you handle things differently?" Hurt and confusion dragged the question from her.

Jake dipped the brush in, loading it with glossy paint, tapping it on the rim, before he answered. "No."

"I see." His answer hurt more than she'd expected.

He threw the brush down into the can. Paint sprayed up onto his jeans. "No, I don't think you do. All things being equal, Sarah, I'd do it exactly the same. I'd have to." He grabbed the rag and scrubbed the floor. Looking up at her, he underlined his refusal. "For Nicholas." He flung the rag away and went back to smoothing paint over weathered boards.

"So." She was halfway down the steps when he gripped her arm.

"Does all that righteous anger feel good, sweetheart? Are you enjoying it?" His chest heaved under his open work shirt. "Must be wonderful to be so absolutely sure that you're the injured party." He glared at her. Tiny flecks of white paint dotted his face and chest. His fingers were white-tipped and crackly with paint.

"Do I look as though I'm enjoying myself?" she spat. "I can't help asking myself what if. You know how it goes. What if you'd disliked me instead of been attracted to me? What if I'd taken to dulling my pain at night with a drink or two? Would you have kept my child from me, then? In all your arrogance would you have decided that I was unfit?" She gulped down the sour bile rising from her empty stomach.

"Stop it, Sarah."

"I can't! That's what keeps me up at night, wondering, wondering what if. What if in all your infinite wisdom you'd decided I didn't meet your standards for parenthood? Parents aren't perfect people. They yell and scream and sometimes make mistakes. And who knows what I might have done, what error of judgment could have sent you rattling off in the night while I never knew you were taking my son with you? For all I know, you probably thought I was running drugs out here."

Dull red mottled the planes of his cheeks.

"Good God. You did." She collapsed into the wicker chair. "I suppose I should be grateful you *ever* decided to tell me the truth." She beat the intricate wicker work in a tattoo of fury.

Jake planted his fists on each arm of the chair and leaned over her, trapping her. "My turn for a question, Sarah. Who are you really angry with? Me? Some corner of that angry, little heart of yours knows my only concern was Nicholas, and I think if you'd been in my shoes you'd have done the same thing." He paused, eyes pinning her to the chair. "Ted? Is all this anger really meant for Ted, who died before you could unleash your outrage on him?"

"I don't have to take this." She struggled to her feet, but Jake crowded closer, pushing her back into the chair.

He tapped her chest right above her heart. "Or are you really angry with yourself? Angry with the Sarah who wasn't all-seeing, all-protective, and so let her child be taken from her? Any of this righteous anger for her?"

"That's a terrible thing to say." She hunched her shoulders.

"But true." His shirt swung open around her, and the sweaty, warm male scent engulfed her. "I know what I did hurt you. I don't excuse myself. But as God is my witness, I'd do it again." Like a battering ram, his words struck her. "I didn't see any other way I could protect Nicholas. I took responsibility for him." The chair slid backward under the force of his shove. "So get your anger untangled, Sarah, before you come dumping it all on me."

Slamming the screen door behind him, he took the stairs in one long stride, calling, "Nicholas! Come here, sport. Sarah and I want to talk to you."

A small tornado, her son charged up the driveway, his bramble-scratched legs pumping for all they were worth. "Coming at you, Jake," he yelled and launched himself into Jake's waiting arms.

Sarah watched Jake's arms go around Nicholas in a comforting squeeze, saw his shaggy, dark head bend to her son. Jake *loved* her son.

"Come inside for a minute, sport." Jake's voice was harsh, but the tenderness he always showed to Nicholas shimmered under curtness.

"My boat's gonna sink." Nicholas slid down Jake's leg. "I hope this is real important."

"It is."

Sarah wondered if she should say anything, but she couldn't. Jake's accusation had stunned her. Was she angry with Ted? With herself? She listened as Jake told a bare-bones version of the events to Nicholas.

"Sarah's my real mom?" Nicholas frowned for a minute. "Or is this some more of that teasing, Jake? 'Cause I already told you I don't like teasing." He poked Jake's chest.

"No one's teasing you, sweetheart," Sarah murmured as Nicholas looked to her. Words stuck in her throat and she didn't know what to say, what to add. Why had Jake decided to tell Nicholas now?

"You love me." Absolute certainty rang in his voice.

"Oh yes," she whispered. "You can't know how much."

"Daddy was wrong, then."

"Yes." She swallowed the tears as she watched Nicholas work out this new development.

"Buck's my cousin, too?"

"Yes." Sarah couldn't look away from the pointy little face with its ridiculously earnest expression.

"I'm gonna stay here?" He stood up and fidgeted. "Me and Jake?"

"I don't know about that, sport." Jake tied Nicholas's shoe laces.

Sarah wondered what Jake was feeling.

"You're going to trip and break your neck one of these days if you don't watch out, kid. Keep an eye on those shoes."

"Listen, Sarah," Nicholas leaned on the chair arm, "me and Jake's a team."

She reached to touch him, but, straightening up as though confident he'd settled the matter, he sprinted out the door and back to his boats.

"Why did you tell him now?" Sarah wrapped her arms around herself to contain the trembling.

"Because I'm sick and tired of the wounded deer look on your face. Because I'm sick to death of hearing you roam this house for hours at night. Yeah, I hear you. I know you're not sleeping." He raked her up and down with a derisory glance as he folded the loose waistband of her shorts. "Not eating." Glaring at her, he swacked the paintbrush on the can and began spreading paint with hard swipes.

"Jake—"

He cut her off. "And don't say 'thank you' in that polite voice you get every now and then." He wiped his face with his shirt tail and turned to the wall. "Now I'm going to be here for the rest of the afternoon painting this damned wall, so you don't have to keep me under observation." Viciously he slapped the brush against the wall. "Go away, Sarah."

The whack of his brush on the boards followed her. She knew some caged emotion was struggling up against its chains. She knew, too, that she had to think about Jake's accusation.

Very quietly she shut the door behind her as she went to join Nicholas. In back of her Jake muttered a low curse.

For several days she and Jake threw themselves into an orgy of cleaning and repairing. At one point as they passed in the hall, Jake lugging a ladder and Sarah carrying rolls of wallpaper, she wondered how much longer they could keep up the pace. Either they would give out, or the house would collapse from an overload of paint.

Nicholas wound between them in cheerful unconcern. He fed F. Roggie, swung on the tree and seemed relatively unaffected by his new status. Every now and then Nicholas would look at Sarah appraisingly or rub his cheek against her leg before bolting off. He ran from dawn to dusk, eating everything Sarah put in front of him and staying stick-thin.

Sarah's jeans and shorts took on an alarming tendency to slide past her hips and with each passing day Jake grew surlier. He never went anywhere with Nicholas, however, without telling her and including her. She always went along. Some part of her now accepted that he wouldn't vanish with Nicholas, but at a deeper level she was no more able to let them take off without her than she could have flapped her arms and flown.

As the days drifted and Jake made no overt moves despite his moodiness, Sarah became less anxious. Gradually, as the corrosive anger drained from her, leaving her limp as seaweed washed up on the shore, she unwound and allowed herself to think about Jake's accusations. For the first time she tried to put herself in his place. What would she have done?

The days drifted on until one morning a blaze of sunlight woke her, and her stomach rumbled with hunger. She found herself smiling. Bright blue sky filled a corner of the window. Stretching in the early morning quiet, she yawned, filled inexplicably with well-being. Lying in sun-warmed sheets, Sarah wondered if maybe she had used Jake as a convenient focus for all the untapped anger she'd felt toward Ted. And, yes, for herself.

Maybe it was guilt and anger that had made her bury herself for so many years. What more, after all, could she have done to save her child? As Sarah watched the sunlight dapple the walls of her newly painted bedroom, she finally forgave herself. She could have done nothing. Nothing.

Scrambling out of bed, she pushed back her hair and shimmied into jeans and a lemon yellow sweater. She was hungry enough to eat anything not nailed down.

"Nicholas? Jake?" She knocked on the bedroom door. No more peering into half-open doors for her. She'd learned her lesson, she thought wryly.

The polished cotton bedspread lay militarily straight, the corners even. Lifting the edge of the curtain near the pillows lying smooth under their shams, a breeze teased her with the sense that someone had just slipped out the window.

In the empty, silent kitchen, a napkin floated to the floor.

"Nicholas!" She ran to the front door.

Jake's truck was gone.

The breeze lifted the oak leaves and stirred the sand underneath.

When Nicholas was playing outside, he left F. Roggie in his container there in the shade.

Sarah walked to the tree and sank onto the crooked swing. There was no sign of the frog. No sign of Nicholas.

Jake must have been waiting for her to let her guard down.

No. That didn't make sense.

Jake had said he could disappear without a trace.

Numb, her hands lying palm up in her lap, she looked around at the peaceful, deserted yard.

Jake wouldn't do that to her.

Like a beginning algebra student, Sarah plodded through simple equations. Jake loved Nicholas. Loving her son, Jake loved some small part of her. If he cared for her, at all, he *could not* deliberately destroy her like this.

Jake knew she wanted him to leave.

He loved Nicholas. He wouldn't leave Nicholas. It would take some unimaginable power to separate Jake from Nicholas.

Sarah stuffed her fist into her mouth to smother the scream tearing from her throat. A whimper escaped.

Jake would not take Nicholas from her. If there were any truth in life, that was it. He would not take her son away from her.

Time lost meaning as she sat in the swing. If she moved, she would bring disaster crashing around her. As long as she didn't move, her world was still whole, not shattered in a million, unrepairable pieces.

Sarah heard the truck first. Then Nicholas's giggle and Jake trumpeting an off-key, slightly bawdy song.

She stood, her muscles as stiff and aching as if she'd run a marathon, blood draining from her head.

From the driveway Jake saw her odd stillness and stopped singing. Uneasy, he slammed on the brakes. What had happened? "Stay here, sport." Vaulting from the truck, Jake ran to her. "Sarah!"

Her face was skim-milk white, and she swayed as he neared her. Damn it to hell, she thought he'd taken Nicholas. "Sarah, I left a note. We went for juice."

"Juice?"

"There wasn't any."

"I thought—" Her eyelids flickered. She was so pale he could see the blue veins.

Jake gripped her shoulders tightly. "I wouldn't have gone without telling you. You know that." He brushed the hair off her face.

"I didn't know where you were." Her voice was thready.

"Didn't you see my note? On the napkin?"

"No."

Sarah straightened her shoulders and breathed deeply.

Thinking she might faint, Jake cupped her neck and bent her forward. "I swear, I wrote where we were going. You were sleeping and I didn't have the heart to wake you. You've been exhausted. I thought you needed sleep. We were only gone twenty minutes, to the 7-Eleven and back."

"Just twenty minutes?" She shook her head. "It seemed so long." In her bleached, white face her lips were blue-gray and pinched. Turning away, she walked toward the swing.

Jake knew they couldn't survive this constant tension and doubt. He'd hoped she would forgive him if he gave her time to think things through. Clearly time hadn't brought trust, much less forgiveness, and he wouldn't be responsible for causing her this kind of anguish any more.

He'd lost.

"Did you phone Buck?" If she had, there was going to be hell to pay.

Her slow steps stopped. "No."

"That's something, I guess." At least she'd believed in him a little. That would be something to remember in the nights to come. He had to leave. He had no other choice. Not any longer. Not after seeing her sick white face when she believed he'd taken off.

"Sarah?"

She turned to face him. "Yes?"

Carefully he touched the soft skin of her throat. One last time, he thought. "I never meant to hurt you. I tried to keep from worrying you."

"I noticed." She twisted the frayed rope ends around her fingers.

Unwinding her hands, Jake raised them to his lips. The skin was cool and smooth. "I'm going to leave. No," he added as her fingers curled under his, "I'm not taking Nicholas from you. I could never do that to you. You should have known." Turning her palms up, he pressed a kiss into them. "I wanted you more than anything life's ever teased me with. But I want your happiness even more." He strode back to the truck.

He was dying inside. Nothing in his life had ever hurt this much. He had to finish before he lost his nerve.

"Hey, sport, come down from there and take a little walk with me. We have to have a talk."

Nicholas tumbled out and then reached back inside for F. Roggie. "Where we going?"

"Down to the lake."

"'kay."

It was harder than he'd imagined. Sitting down on the dock, Jake tugged Nicholas over to him. "Listen, sport, you know your dad wanted me to bring you back to America, right?"

"Yeah." Nicholas tossed a stick into the water that shone clear in the sunshine. Minnows zigged where the stick splashed.

"Well, you're here now, where you belong."

"Yeah, I like it a real lot, Jake. It's swell, all of us here." Nicholas belly flopped onto the dock and looked down into the water.

"That's the problem. I don't belong here." Jake cleared his throat. "This is your home." He placed his hand on Nicholas's back, feeling the bony spine under his fingers. Darn kid. Couldn't put an ounce on him. "Not mine."

"'Course it's your home, Jake," Nicholas scoffed, looking back over his shoulder. "Me and you are a team. I explained all that to Sarah."

"It's not that simple for grown-ups, Nicholas." Jake rubbed Nicholas's head brusquely.

"You're teasing, right?" Anxiety darkened Nicholas's eyes.

"No." Jake cleared his throat again. He couldn't swallow.

"You promised you'd never leave me, Jake! You promised!" Nicholas scrambled to his feet and stood over Jake. "You can't go back on a promise."

"I have to leave."

"Then I'm gonna go with you." Nicholas plopped onto Jake's lap and hung an arm around his neck. "You don't get along so good without me, Jake. You get scared of lightning and stuff. And I can help now that I know stuff like fishing." He searched Jake's face eagerly. "'kay?"

"No."

"You can't go without me, Jake."

"You have to stay, Nicholas. You'll be going to school, you have to take care of F. Roggie. He can't go where I'm going, you know." Jake wrapped his arms around the scrawny little body. "And Sarah needs you, too. Think how lonely she'd be without you."

"You'll be lonely, too, Jake," Nicholas said tearfully, burying his head on Jake's shoulder.

"Yeah."

"Don't leave, Jake. I love you." Nicholas's tears were soaking Jake's shirt.

Jake swallowed the hot lump in his throat. "I have to leave, and you have to be strong and help Sarah and study hard." Jake couldn't go on. Lowering his head over Nicholas he fought for control. He rubbed his face against the shining softness of Nicholas's hair, so like Sarah's, and refused to think of how close he'd come to happiness. "Nicholas, I can't stay."

He stood up and carried the weeping boy in his arms back to Sarah.

Her eyes were enormous in her pale face and Jake looked at the two people he loved more than anything on earth and wished the ground would open up right then and close over him. He couldn't leave them.

He couldn't stay.

While Jake shoved stuff into his bag, Nicholas clung to him and wept uncontrollably, eyes puffy and swollen. Like a ghost, Sarah tagged behind, the blue of her eyes deep and glittery. He almost grabbed her and kissed her hard when he saw the misery on her face, misery he had caused and was trying the best he could to erase. But he was afraid if he kissed her he'd never be able to leave.

At the last moment, Jake thought Sarah was going to say something.

She was clutching Nicholas to her as if her life depended on it. Nicholas's sobs shook his body and Sarah patted his back as she looked at Jake. He thought her lips were trembling.

He waited. Glacier ice was bearing down on him and her yellow blouse was like the dying sun. She didn't speak. Finally he shrugged and went up to her. "Sarah, I'm losing everything I ever wanted in this life, but I'd still do things the same way."

She blinked.

"And, yes, I think I know what love is now. I never knew anything could hurt so much. I said once that I'd never hurt you, but all I seem to have done is cause you heartache. You told me that pain's part of life, but God help me, I can't live with what I'm doing to you."

Tracing the contours of her face, the soft chin, the sweet forehead, Jake memorized Sarah, her shape, her texture.

He stooped to enclose her and Nicholas in his arms, enclosing them with all the love he'd never given before. Lightly Jake touched a spot above her left breast. "There's my home, Sarah, the only one I've ever wanted."

He wouldn't look back. Starting the rackety engine, he kept telling himself not to look back at Sarah and Nicholas and the house. But he looked in the rearview mirror and saw Nicholas tear loose from Sarah's arms and run down the driveway after him.

"Jake, don't go! Don't go!"

Jake's truck turning onto the highway snapped Sarah out of the strange immobility she'd been in since she found her house empty. Why hadn't she stopped Jake? Why had she indulged herself in the luxury of anger and hurt? She waited for Nicholas to trudge back to her.

"Sarah, I want Jake to come back." He rubbed his eyes, leaving streaks of dirt.

"Me too, honey."

Too late she realized what her anger had blinded her from seeing. She loved Jake and she'd let him go. Sarah wanted to sob right along with Nicholas. Instead, she picked him up and carried him home.

Night came, and the house seemed empty. Sarah wandered through the halls conjuring up Jake in every room. In Jake's bed, Nicholas woke up screaming there were monsters in the closet. Trying to calm him, she opened the door and showed him there was nothing there.

Except there was. A flat, purple-and-white striped box was tucked into the corner. Reluctantly Sarah brought it out and opened it.

A froth of Egyptian cotton and Irish linen erupted. The white blouse with its delicate tucks and cobweb lightness spilled into her hands. A courting blouse if she'd ever seen one, Sarah thought, bursting into sobs. When had Jake bought the blouse? What moment had he been waiting for? She rocked back and forth, tears splattering the pristine white as she curled up on a pillow next to Nicholas, Jake's pillow.

A week went by. Sarah and Nicholas clung to each other in silent comfort, not talking about Jake. Sarah called Buck and asked him to do the necessary legal work so that she could enroll Nicholas in school, come September. Being Buck, he had to know the whole story, and afterwards said only, "Hang in there, Sairy, you'll be okay."

Sarah knew she'd be okay. That wasn't the problem. The problem was that she missed Jake. She missed the small incursions into her space. She'd come to depend on the perking of her blood when he touched her. She missed his touch with every fiber of her being. If she'd known where to find him, she'd have dragged him back by his devil-black hair.

There weren't any closets to clean, no rooms to paint. Sarah kept thinking she saw Jake just out of the corner of her eye and she'd turn quickly, but of course he wasn't there.

he and Nicholas stayed outdoors until dark drove them
side. Outside, Jake's presence didn't haunt them.

Accepting that she couldn't keep up a guide schedule once
Nicholas started school, Sarah applied for a job with the
newspaper. When Bernice Christianson called to tell her she
ould start in August, Sarah breathed a sigh of relief. At
ast that problem had solved itself. She'd never used any of
he money she'd received from Ted's insurance, and now she
ransferred it to a trust fund for Nicholas.

Life went on. Nicholas seldom left her side, carting F.
oggie everywhere. Sarah grew used to the frog sitting in
ake's place on the table at breakfast, lunch and dinner, a
quat, green, poor substitute for a prince.

Chapter Eleven

At the Buckhead Marina Tavern, Jake held up a finger the bartender. "Hit me," he said, lining up the bottles front of him and blearily counting them off, each one symbol of the mistakes he'd made with Sarah.

Jolly shook his head but sent another beer sliding dow the cypress-wood counter. The door opened. Sarah's cousi ambled in and lowered himself onto a bar stool, one le hooked onto the rung.

Had Sarah sent him? Jake narrowed his eyes and peere at Buck through the cigarette smoke before tilting the brow bottle to his lips and downing half of it. Probably not.

"Evening, Donnelly." Buck gestured to Jolly to bring hi a beer.

"Again, Jolly." Jake waggled his hand.

"Lot of bottles there," Buck commented, tipping h cowboy hat back.

"Yeah." Jake glowered. "What of it?" He half stoo spoiling for a good fight and no one better than Buck to l

oose on. Maybe a good fight would ease the pain in his
eart. "Come on outside."

"Whoa, big guy." Buck leaned back. He measured Jake
p and down. "Even two days into a pie-eyed drunk, you're
ut of my league."

"Five days, and it's still early in the evening," Jake mut-
:red, tilting the bottle to the light and studying the shining
olor, color that shone like Sarah's hair in sunshine.

"Like it around here, do you? I hear you've been check-
ıg with some agricultural-engineering big shots from the
niversity. Got some fancy plans for working on the lake?"

"Nope." Jake didn't want to be reminded of dreams.

"Can't leave, stud?"

"Can't stay." Jake took a long swallow, hoping for
orgetfulness.

"So how long you planning to camp out in your truck
ack in the Glades?" Buck's drawl stretched out into the
pace between them. "Some of my buddies spotted you a
ouple of days ago, said you hit the Buckhead every night."

"What's it to you?" Jake growled.

"Nothing to me." Buck swirled the beer in his bottle.
Maybe a lot to somebody I'm right fond of."

Sarah. Jake concentrated on Buck. "Cut the good-old-
oy bit, Reilly. Get to the point."

"Right." Buck leaned his elbows on the bar and rolled his
ottle between his palms. "You win the prize for plain
umb, Donnelly. Sarah's up at the house crying her eyes
ut, you're here drinking yourself into a stupor."

"She tell you what I did?" Jake eyed his empty bottle.

"Sure."

"I hurt her. I kept hurting her. No matter what I did, I
ade everything worse." Jake started to raise his hand once
ore.

"True." Pushing Jake's arm down, Buck shook his head
t Jolly. "But you don't look very happy, and Sarah sure

isn't. Nicholas, of course," Buck added sarcastically, "is a
happy as a pig in a mud wallow. But he misses you, too."

"I hurt her."

"Yeah, yeah, you said that. But Sarah doesn't hol
grudges and I never figured you for a quitter." Buck looked
at him in disgust.

Jake dredged up a smile. "Nice work, fella. You're hit
ting all the buttons. Trouble is, I've got a couple of years o
you and I know the routine."

"Figured you did," Buck laughed. "It's the biggest dam
mess I ever heard, I'll give you that. I can't imagine wha
strings you pulled to get papers on Nicholas. Some fanc
footwork sneaking him out of there, I reckon."

"Yeah." Jake remembered how close it had been at th
end, getting the oil exec out first, because Ted wasn't read
to let Nicholas go, and then going back in on a lightnin
strike for Nicholas and trying to time everything so he coul
get to the kid before Ted died and left him unprotected
"Yeah."

"And you're backing off from an itty-bitty thing lik
Sarah?" Buck snorted. "Not what I'd expect of a move
and shaker like you."

Jake menaced him with a surly glance.

"Stuff it, Donnelly. Of course I researched you. I kno
your history. You're the guy they call in to solve the dead
end problems. And you always do, so I was told. You hadn'
been in Sarah's house twenty-four hours before I had yo
scoped out. You don't think I'd have let you stay ther
otherwise, do you?" Buck's sly grin mocked him.

Jake looked right back with a tight smile. "Think yo
could have shaken me loose from there before I was goo
and ready?" He flexed his hands.

Buck laughed. "Guess not, but that kind of threat usu
ally works. No, I'm not crazy enough to get in the way o
you and something you've set your sights on. You can eas
off, Donnelly. I'm not here to punch you out. Even if

:ould," Buck said, looking at Jake's bulk and width. "Not
:hat I wouldn't *like* to punch out your lights, you understand, but Sarah would skin me alive if I did."

"She know you're here?" Jake tried to suppress the hope
:hat rose in him.

"No. Not going to tell her, either."

"Fine by me." Jake flipped his wallet open and laid
money on the bar. "Now leave me alone. I've got some real
drinking to do."

Buck pocketed the money. "Nope, buddy, you're
:hrough. You're not the solitary-drunk type. What you are
s an old-time romantic. Well, Donnelly, life's real and full
of pain a lot of times. Sarah loves you. You love her. You
guys can work it out from there. That's what life is all
about, tough guy, not making noble gestures and disappearing into the sunset."

"I can see you in a courtroom, Reilly. I'll bet you don't
ose many cases." Jake remarked, lightness bubbling
:hrough him.

"One. A long time ago." Buck's modest grin was regret-
ul. "Now, what you're going to do is shave, shower and
sober up."

Jake held out a steady hand. "Sober as a judge."

"Okay, just don't sit in on any of my cases," Buck said,
nis heels thumping the floor as he stood. "You sober enough
:o drive?"

"Nope." Jake laughed, springtime warmth tickling his
blood.

"Damn. Come on, Donnelly, we've got work to do, and
since I've kinda been thinking of you as family, anyway, let
me tell you about this job I heard about that could use your
talents. Well, not quite all of them . . ."

Sarah curled up on the sofa. Roaming the empty rooms
f her home, she usually wound up here. Moonlight silvered

the oak leaves and sand. Through her open door the breeze
waltzed in.

Off in the distance, she heard a truck. Her heart rat-a-tat
tatted like a frenzied snare drummer. She turned the yellow
porch light on and watched a shiny pickup crawl slowly up
the driveway.

Jake saw the open door and the yellow porch light. Anxiety tightened his grip on the wheel. Maybe Buck had been
wrong. Could Sarah forgive him? Could they have a future? Not if he sat here forever just watching that empty
doorway, that's for sure. He turned off the engine and took
a deep breath.

Watching, Sarah's shoulders drooped. Not Jake's old
truck.

The cab door banged behind the large, solid man who
stepped down. Moonlight shadowed him, lay on his dark
hair. He reached into a tool case he carried and walked to
the crooked swing, his powerful thighs moving smoothly
and familiarly under low-riding jeans.

"Jake?" Sarah whispered.

Pounding on the wooden slat, the man loosened it. More
pounding.

"Jake!" Sarah screamed. Barefoot, nightgowned and
moonmad, she tore out of the house. "Jake!"

Jake turned, dropping the hammer as Sarah, a warm,
sweet-smelling Sarah who clouded his senses, catapulted
into his waiting arms. Her legs locked around his waist and
Jake trembled with the force of his wanting and love and
Sarah.

"You fool, you hardheaded nincompoop, you stubborn
idiot, why did you leave?" She wept and laughed into his
ear.

"Sarah, you do say the sweetest things," he said, his lips
moving feverishly over her skin, nipping, tasting. His hands
swept over her, restlessly touching, stroking. She was in his
arms, at last, after all the lonely nights dreaming about her.

"Oh, you crazy man, I love you, I love you." Sarah ran her fingers through his hair, over his wide shoulders. He'd come back. "Are you really here? And what are you doing with the swing? And a new truck?"

"First things first."

His kiss silenced her and Sarah strained against Jake, needing him desperately. Held by him, she regretted the pride and stubbornness that had let him disappear out of her life.

"Jake, you were right, I *was* taking out my long-buried anger against Ted, and, yes, against myself, on you, but you left before I understood that." She pulled his shirt out of his jeans and ran her hands up skin that quivered at her touch. Such power she had over this strong male.

"I was wrong, too. I left because you couldn't ever trust me again." He pulled her tightly against him.

"But I did trust you! I knew somehow you wouldn't take Nicholas, that's why I didn't call Buck. I worked it out." Sarah knew she had to convince Jake. "See, I know you love Nicholas, and I was terrified that you wouldn't be able to leave without him. But I finally realized that your love for him was all mixed in with your feelings for me, just as mine were for you." Sarah cradled his face in her palms, his skin smooth against her. "You shaved," she said, tears choking her.

He nuzzled his cheek against her. "Had to. If I was coming courting again."

The tears slid down her face. She'd almost thrown all this away. "Oh, Jake, I guess we're a package deal, the three of us. I love you for the way you are with me, I love you because of the way you care for Nicholas—I don't know, it's all so confusing, but I want you with us." She placed his head against her heart. "Come home, Jake."

"I'll never hurt you again, Sarah," Jake said fiercely.

"Of course you will. And I'll hurt you. But we'll work through it. You may be my hero," she brushed her lips over his, tasting the salt of her tears, "but life's not a fairy tale. Whatever happens, we'll survive it as long as we're together."

His lips took hers in a long kiss of promise that robbed her of breath and dried her tears with the heat of her need for this man, this one man who'd come to her in darkness and freed her. Finally, Sarah stroked his chest. "You never answered my questions."

"Yeah, I forgot," he smiled and held her hand over his hard-pumping heart. "I fixed your swing. I bought a new truck because I'm going to need it on my new job as agricultural consulting engineer and I needed a safe car for my family."

Sarah inhaled.

"You are going to marry me, aren't you, Sarah? Note that I'm asking, not telling." He whirled her in huge circles, his laugh mingling with hers until they toppled into the night damp sand, giddy with laughter, legs and arms tangled together.

Sarah looked at him. He was the man who'd torn down the walls she'd built, hauled her out from behind them and enraged her into life. He was the man who'd given her her son back. He was the man whose touch stirred the deepest feminine side of her in a way no one ever had before.

"Of course I'll marry you, idiot," she scolded, nipping his ear.

"Jake!"

At Nicholas's yell, Jake sat up, holding Sarah close to him. She leaned her head against his chest, loving the sound of his heart beating under her.

"You're home!" Nicholas hurled himself at them and tumbled them all back into the sand. "I knew you'd come back, I knew it! You wouldn't break a promise."

Jake put his free arm around Nicholas and squeezed him. "Not if I could help it, I wouldn't."

Nicholas looked at Sarah. "You're outside in your nightgown." He looked at the moon and the ground. "It's night and we're all sitting in the sand. I like this." He nodded with satisfaction.

"Me, too, sport," Jake said, swinging Nicholas up onto his shoulders and pulling Sarah closer. "But let's go in, okay?"

Arm in arm, Sarah walked with Jake toward the beckoning yellow porch light. The leveled swing swayed in the breeze and behind them she saw the moon cast their shadows forward, forming a bridge from her, Jake and Nicholas to the old house welcoming them home.

* * * * *

**A compelling novel of deadly revenge and passion
from bestselling international
romance author Penny Jordan**

POWER
PLAY

Eleven years had passed but the
terror of that night was something
Pepper Minesse would never
forget. Fueled by revenge against
the four men who had brutally
shattered her past, she set in
motion a deadly plan to destroy
their futures.

Available in February!

Penny
Jordan

Silhouette Romances®

Diana Palmer brings you an Award of Excellence title... and the first Silhouette Romance DIAMOND JUBILEE book.

ETHAN
by Diana Palmer

In January 1990, Diana Palmer continues her bestselling LONG, TALL TEXANS series with *Ethan*— the story of a rugged rancher who refuses to get roped and tied by Arabella Craig, the one woman he can't resist.

The Award of Excellence is given to one specially selected title per month. Spend January with *Ethan* #694 ... a special DIAMOND JUBILEE title ... only in Silhouette Romance.